ROMANCE-ology 101

Bookmark: Copyright
Published by Julie Lessman, LLC.
Copyright 2013. Julie Lessman, LLC.
Cover by Lessmark, LLC
ISBN: 1490955771
ISBN-13: 9781490955773

Excerpts from Revell are used by permission for each of the following books:
Julie Lessman, *A Passion Most Pure*, Revell, a division of Baker Publishing Group, copyright 2008.
Julie Lessman, *A Passion Redeemed*, Revell, a division of Baker Publishing Group, copyright 2008.
Julie Lessman, *A Passion Denied*, Revell, a division of Baker Publishing Group, copyright 2008.
Julie Lessman, *A Hope Undaunted*, Revell, a division of Baker Publishing Group, copyright 2010.
Julie Lessman, *A Heart Revealed*, Revell, a division of Baker Publishing Group, copyright 2011.
Julie Lessman, *A Love Surrendered*, Revell, a division of Baker Publishing Group, copyright 2012.
Julie Lessman, *Love at Any Cost*, Revell, a division of Baker Publishing Group, copyright 2013.
Julie Lessman, *Dare to Love Again*, Revell, a division of Baker Publishing Group, copyright 2014.

ROMANCE-ology 101:

Writing Romantic Tension for the Inspirational and Sweet Markets

Julie Lessman

Julie Lessman, LLC
2013

Dedication

My deepest thanks to Revell Publishing for
allowing me the use of all excerpts utilized in this book.

To The Seekers—friends and authors extraordinaire:
Mary Connealy, Janet Dean, Debby Giusti, Audra Harders,
Ruth Logan Herne, Pam Hillman, Cara Lynn James, Myra Johnson,
Glynna Kaye, Sandra Leesmith, Tina Radcliffe, and Missy Tippens.
I treasure both you and the awesome God
Who brought us all together.

And to Vince Mooney—the Seeker friend responsible
for me writing this book—your brilliant mind
never ceases to amaze me.

Table of Contents

Introduction

A KISS IS *NOT* JUST A KISS
Tips to Escalate Romantic Tension

CRACK! Okay, people, sit up straight, hands on the desk, and cell phones off. My name is Mrs. Lessman and playtime is *O-V-E-R*. The new semester begins today and you may as well know right off the ruler that this is no chump course, got it?

Good. Because as a die-hard advocate of Romance-ology, there's nothing more annoying than a pupil who doesn't give his or her all to *the* major component in a romance novel: the kiss.

I mean, heaven forbid! Would *Gone with the Wind* be the same if Rhett gave Scarlett a handshake on top of that dusky hill? Of course not! Would Ryan Gosling give you palpitations if he pushed Rachel McAdams to the wall in *The Notebook* to save her from a falling ceiling? *Puh-leez!* Oh sure, and I suppose the sigh factor would go through the roof if George Peppard kissed the cat in the rain instead of Audrey Hepburn in *Breakfast at Tiffany's*!

Come on, people, this is romance, not women's fiction . . . which means the kiss matters. *A lot!* And contrary to Mr. Herman Hupfeld in his song *As Time Goes By*, a kiss is *not* just a kiss nor is a sigh just a sigh. No, ma'am, a kiss oughta make you tingle to the tips of your curled toes . . . just like in the movies.

Julie Lessman

Now, does this mean that a bona fide lip lock is the only way to up romantic tension? Absolutely not. Romantic tension can be just as high with the non-kiss or the almost kiss, so don't get your knickers in a knot. But one thing is for dead sure, whether a kiss takes place or not—romantic tension does hover around the "hope" of a kiss. A hope grounded in a God-given longing to be loved, and a hope instilled by the very God who created passion. Why? Because passion is important! Not just to romance readers, but to everyone on the planet. We were created that way by a passionate God who analogizes His own depth of love for us in a very passionate love letter called "Song of Solomon."

BANG! Miss Carol Moncado, spit that chocolate out right now . . .

So listen up, everybody. Anybody can warm up the pages with blatant bedroom scenes, but it takes a real pro to heighten the romantic tension in a book with only a look . . . a kiss . . . or even a non-kiss. In the following pages, you'll learn tried-and-true tips on how to do that, along with some truly unique kisses that are tame enough for the inspirational/sweet markets, but romantic enough to raise the sigh factor. Of course, Principal Mooney insisted we utilize excerpts from my books, so what could I do but acquiesce? After all, the man signs my paycheck!

KA-POW! Miss Andie Tubbs—two demerits for shooting spit wads, and put that pea gun away!

All right, students—shoulders straight, eyes on the board, and Miss Amber Perry, your hair looks lovely, so I suggest you put the comb and mirror away, capiche?

On your mark, get set . . . PUCKER UP!

Chapter 1

Getting Inside the Hero's Head with Internal Monologue

Okay, class, raise your hand if you think the heroine is the most important feature in a romance novel. **CRACK!!** Well, you're wrong, people, because it's not the heroine who lures over 74.8 million people to read at least one romance novel a year (source: RWA Reader Survey 2008). Nope, it's that big, strong, hulking-male-type who tempts the female readers (*ahem* … women account for 91 percent of sales) to lay down their hard-earned cash for a little bit of romance.

Why? Because each female reader IS the heroine in her own eyes, exploring the bonds of love and romance vicariously through the heroine in any romance novel. A woman who just wants to be loved like the hero loves the heroine.

Let's face it—the male is key. His feelings/reactions revealed through his "internal monologue" (i.e., his thoughts) generate readers' feelings/reactions even more so than the heroine's because *his* desire translates into the desire every woman wishes she could elicit.

In this scene from book 3 of my Winds of Change series, *A Love Surrendered,* Luke McGee just discovers his wife, Katie, is secretly being tutored by her former fiancé and determines to coerce a confession. The first example is the beginning of the scene from Katie's point of view (POV) to give you a sense of how much tension you're missing without the male POV, and then the second is the entire clip through Luke's POV. After you read both, try to imagine the entire scene in the heroine's POV instead, and I'll bet you seven chocolate kisses from the teacher's candy jar that the romance—and the tension—would not be near as palpable!

HEROINE'S POV

Katie tensed when he flipped off the light and crawled into bed, pulling her close. To deflect her guilt over studying with Jack, she trailed a finger over Luke's bicep and down his arm, slowly circling his palm with her thumb.

With a gentle kiss to her hair, he snuggled close. "So … what have you and Kit been doing with your evenings?"

Her thumb ceased and she swallowed hard, unwilling to divulge that her ex-fiancé was secretly tutoring her. No, not yet, not with an exam next week. She forced a casual tone. "Oh, nothing much, lots of books, games, walks—you know, the usual."

He paused, fiddling with the strap of her gown. "So you just stayed home all week? Didn't go anywhere else, like your parents' or Lizzie's?"

A knot of guilt dipped in her throat. "Well, I did go out last night," she said quickly, voice breathless. "Mother watched Kit while I studied at the law library."

"Alone?" he asked, tone innocent while he grazed her lips with a gentle kiss.

She hesitated, unwilling to lie. "Yes, of course. Meg couldn't go."

"Aw, you hate studying alone." He massaged her arm. "Run into anybody you know?"

Icy needles prickled her skin. "Uh ... yeah." She rushed to kiss him full on the mouth, hoping to sway him in a different direction. "Mmm ..."

He returned her passion with low groan, kissing her thoroughly before trailing his lips to her throat. "Who?"

She moaned softly, ignoring his question while she tunneled fingers into his hair.

"Who, Katie?" he asked again, and her body went completely still. Her mouth opened and closed, but nothing came out, eyes blinking so fast, she thought she might cry.

HERO'S POV

He flipped off the light and crawled into bed, pulling her close. She trailed a finger over his bicep and down his arm, slowly circling his palm with her thumb. With a gentle kiss to her head, he exhaled his stress, praying the encounter with Jack was only by chance. "So ... what have you and Kit been doing with your evenings?"

Her thumb ceased. "Nothing much, lots of books, games, walks—you know, the usual."

He paused, fiddling with the strap of her gown. "You just stayed home all week? Didn't go anywhere else, like your parents' or Lizzie's?"

Her chest expanded and released with a heavy draw of air before she responded. "Well, I did go out last night," she said slowly, voice breathless. "Mother watched Kit while I studied at the law library."

The air eased from his lungs. "Alone?"

She hesitated a moment too long. "Yes, of course. Meg couldn't go."

"Aw, you hate studying alone." He massaged her arm, his jaw suddenly tight. "Run into anybody you know?"

He felt the shift of her throat when she swallowed hard. "Uh ... yeah." She rushed to kiss him full on the mouth, swaying her lips against his. "Mmm ..."

Heat jolted, and he rolled her over, kissing her thoroughly before trailing his lips to her throat. "Who?" he whispered, the scent of her almost making him forget that he cared.

She moaned softly, ignoring his question while she tunneled fingers into his hair. His lips wandered lower. "Who, Katie?" he asked again, and her body went completely still. He looked up, heart thundering. *Tell me the truth, Katie—please.* "You all right?" he asked quietly.

Her mouth opened and closed as if she wanted to speak, but nothing came out, blue eyes blinking so fast, he thought she might cry. *Please, Katie, don't lie ...*

"Luke," she began with a chew of her lip, "you know how I've struggled with Contract Law and you've been too busy to help?" She avoided his eyes. "Well, I ..." A shaky breath quivered out. "Accepted someone's offer to tutor."

He didn't breathe.

Disappointment stabbed when she lunged to take his mouth with hers, pulling him down. "I love you, Luke," she whispered, "and I missed you so much, it hurt."

Yeah, I know the feeling. Tempering his frustration, he gently fondled her lips, taking his time with a languid kiss that made her go soft beneath his hold. In a slow and measured tease, he explored her mouth with his own, eliciting a moan deep in her throat when he gently tugged at her lip. "Who?" he whispered again, mouth straying to the lobe of her ear.

"What?" Her eyes were closed and her breathing shallow.

His mouth meandered the curve of her neck, keeping pace with his hands as they skimmed the curve of her body. "I was wondering who helped you?"

She tensed beneath his lips and he knew this was it—the moment of reckoning. When Katie would tell him the truth or lie through her teeth. Taut with both passion and anger, Luke coaxed, trailing her collarbone with kisses while toying with the strap of her gown …

She shuddered beneath his lips, voice barely audible and as soft as a guilty thought. "Jack."

His lips stilled on her skin. The lids of his eyes weighted down with relief before heat surged that had nothing to do with the lure of his wife's body. "Jack?" he rasped, the word more of a hiss than a name. He jerked to a sitting position, shocked at the venom that flowed in his veins. "You asked *Jack* to tutor you?"

Wincing, she shot up, hand clutched to his arm. "But you told me to get help …"

His mouth went slack. "From your *teachers*, Katie Rose," he ground out, "not your former fiancé."

❧❦

A love story is *never* just about one person, it's about two, so sometimes it's important to round out critical scenes with both POVs, which we'll expound upon later in chapter 4, "Utilizing Dual Point of View." But for now, the intent of the following scene is to demonstrate how romantic tension climbs when we see the scene through the male POV.

In this scene from *A Passion Denied*, the subordinate hero Patrick O'Connor has been sleeping at the *Herald* for over a month due to an awful fight with his wife that has embittered him. The subordinate heroine, his wife, Marcy, has done everything in her power to heal the rift—prayer, forgiveness, kindness, and patience—all to no avail. Following a tense fight, she finally turns on him, ready to embrace bitterness herself … until God speaks to her heart and convinces her to forgive *one more time*.

She does so by bringing her husband the clean clothes he would need when he leaves to spend the night at the *Herald*. When she does, the POV switches to Patrick's, and through his eyes, we see a miracle wrought in his soul, something that would be lost if the POV were only Marcy's.

She tried to breathe, but the air was too thick, panting from her lips in a faint, feeble rasp. She pressed a hand to her chest, tight with the burden of decision. A choice. To lay down her pride and forgive. Or to embrace the hurt and strike back. Obedience or sin. She squeezed her eyes shut, torn by the prompting of the Spirit and the pull of her flesh. *Oh, God, I can't! Help me, please …*

Thoughts pelted her brain. Patrick's cruelty. His indifference. His rejection.

She put her palms to her ears, desperate to shut them out. "No! I choose to forgive." Gasping for air, she staggered from the bed, her mind set on a course that would cost her her pride. She groped for the light, then shielded her eyes from the glare, lips moving in silent prayer. Her pulse raced while she gathered his things—a clean shirt, pressed trousers, and a favorite tie. She bundled them in her arms. The scent of him rose, sweet to her senses, and her heart flooded with hope, purging the grief he had caused.

"Oh, God, help me …," she whispered. Her breathing became deeper, unrestricted as she moved to the bureau. By God, he would have clean socks and underwear.

And she would have a clean heart.

Her pulse beat steady and strong as she padded down the stairs, no longer afraid of the light in the hall or the stranger in the parlor. She drew in a deep breath.

Perfect love casts out fear.

He seemed so haggard as she entered the room, and her heart longed to hold him. Instead, she placed his things on the couch, grieved at the anger she still saw in his eyes. She looked away, unable to bear it. "Forgive me, Patrick, for losing my temper. I love you …and I will forever."

She moved to the door, suddenly spent, pausing only to speak over her shoulder. "Good night, my love. Please get some sleep."

And without another word, she returned to their room and silently dressed for bed. When she laid her head on the pillow, it wasn't to sleep. No, it was first to pray, and then to weep. Because she knew, all too well. *The prayer of a righteous man availeth much.*

—

He stared at the empty door, unable to comprehend the love he'd just seen. His pulse droned in his ears as he slumped in the chair, body buzzing and mind numb.

She'd forgiven in the face of her anger. He dropped his head in his hands. In total obedience to God.

Unlike him.

And total love for the man who spurned her.

Wetness welled in his eyes and he choked on a sob. An aching realization stabbed within, but its pain was kind, unlike the agony of guilt. Conviction lifted the blindness from his eyes, and he knew he had failed. He'd turned his back on God as well as his wife. And for what? Wounded pride that had yielded nothing but his demise. And hers.

Two souls for the price of one sin.

He heaved with pain, barely able to breathe. His mind grappled for the verse Mitch had given him. He closed his eyes and it suddenly pierced his thoughts, allowing a sliver of light to shatter the darkness.

The law of Jehovah is perfect, restoring the soul.

Oh, God, the law. To forgive. Could he really do it?

He opened his eyes in shock, revelation prickling his spine.

The law is perfect. Like God's love, Patrick thought, and hope surged in his chest.

He thought of Marcy, and for the first time in weeks, he could see her clearly, unscathed by his anger. A woman, pure of heart and strong of character, loving God while loving him. He thought of the damage he'd done, and his heart fisted in grief. *Oh, God, forgive me—I don't deserve her.*

He leapt to his feet, sin no longer weighting him down, and bounded the steps, two at a time. The hall was dark, but his step was light, and he prayed for mercy as never before. He neared their room and could hear her weeping, muffled and wrenching his heart like it should. He stopped in the doorway, staggered by what he'd done, and watched as their bed shivered with her grief. She didn't hear him until he knelt by her side, and when he spoke, she jerked in surprise. "Marcy . . ."

The hitch of her breath was harsh in the dark.

He pressed a hand to her wet cheek, sick inside at the pain he'd caused. "God knows I don't deserve it, but can you . . . will you . . . forgive me for being a fool?"

❧❦

So . . . the take-home factor here is the male POV always ramps up the romantic tension in a story because a reader—just like the heroine—wants to know what the hero is thinking, feeling, and hiding. To sum it up—it's wise to incorporate a fair amount of male POV in a romance novel where the reader gets to one-up the heroine with a pulse-pounding glimpse into the hero's head.

Chapter 2

Maximizing Use of Beats in Dialogue

Okay, class . . . today, instead of "he said, she said," we're going to focus on the "he did, she did" aspect of dialogue, because as the old adage goes, "Action speaks louder than words." And as a teacher, it's been my experience that in a classroom, action with a ruler speaks louder than anything.

THWACK!

Eyes on the board, people, because I'm going to show you just how much action beats can heat up a scene by ramping up the romantic tension. Instead of overuse of speaker attributions (i.e., he said, she said), try mixing it up with a healthy dose of action beats and fewer speaker attributions.

In scenes that require tension, I have found I prefer using **straight action beats alone** instead of a combination of speaker attributions and beats. I think it enhances the drama, especially when you only have two speakers, allowing less chance for confusion.

Here is an excerpt from *A Hope Undaunted* between hero Luke McGee and heroine Katie O'Connor that shows it both ways—first with speaker attributions *and* beats, and then with beats only, which I prefer because I think it elicits more tension. But . . . *you* be the judge!

SPEAKER ATTRIBUTION/BEATS EXAMPLE

"Is that all this was between us then?" he said, locking her wrist midair when she tried to slap him. "A little fun while your rich boyfriend was off limits?"

"I never started any of this," she said, jerking her hand free, "and you know it. It was you."

"No," he said, his fingers digging into her arms as he pressed her to the counter. "But you sure finished it, didn't you?"

ACTION BEATS ONLY (teacher's preference)

She tried to slap him, but he locked her wrist midair with a painful grip. "Is that all this was between us then? A little fun while your rich boyfriend was off limits?"

She jerked her hand free. "I never started any of this, and you know it. It was you."

His fingers dug into her arms as he pressed her to the counter. "No, but you sure finished it, didn't you?"

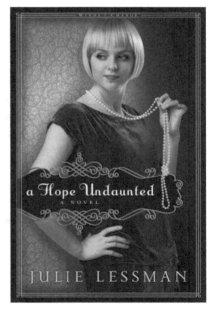

☙ ❧

In the following angry love scene between hero Collin McGuire and heroine Faith O'Connor from *A Passion Most Pure*, I relied heavily on beats (all underlined to point them out) instead of speaker attributions because for me, speaker attributions can often slow the flow of a tense scene. I did use two speaker attributions at the end, which are both **bolded** below, but only because I wanted a strong response, such as Faith "screaming" or Collin speaking "quietly," two dramatic effects I needed to drive the emotion home.

She jerked her hand from his and stood, quivering as she caved against the chair. "I can't marry you, Collin."

He leaned in. "I know you love me. Can you deny it?"

She didn't speak, and he jumped up and rounded the table, gripping her arms to lift her to her feet. When she wouldn't look at him, he grabbed her chin and forced her. "Look at me! Can you deny you love me?"

She stared at him through a mist of tears. "Let me go, you're hurting my arm."

"Tell me you don't love me."

"I don't love you."

"You're lying, Faith. I would have thought better of you than that."

"Well don't!" **she screamed**. "I'm not better than that. You've said your apologies, Collin, now let me go."

She tried to turn away. He jerked her back. "I know you love me. Don't you think I can feel it every time I touch you?" He pulled her to him, and she cried out before his lips silenced her with a savage kiss. She struggled to pull free, but he only held her tighter, the blood pounding in his brain. His mouth was everywhere—her throat, her earlobes, her lips—and he could feel the heat coming in waves as she melted against him. She was quivering when he finally let her go.

"You love me, Faith," **he said quietly**. "You know that, and I know that. Your heart belongs to me, and nothing can ever change that fact—not Charity, not you, and not your god."

☙◦❧

I hope these two examples shed some light on just how important "beats" are, not only to good dialogue, but in escalating the romantic tension in a novel as well. In fact, beats are the heart and soul of what I call "movie mind," or dialogue that plays like a movie in the reader's mind. For more info on "movie mind," see my *Seekerville* blog entitled, Keeping It "Reel" … Or a "Novel" Approach to Putting a Movie in Your Reader's Mind at http://seekerville.blogspot.com/2013/03/keeping-it-reel-or-novel-approach-to.html.

Okay, everybody ready? Start humming "And the beat goes on … and the beat goes on …"

Chapter 3

Effectively Using Dialogue to Escalate Tension

As you'll discover in chapter 5, anger is a powerful component in escalating romantic tension, and dialogue is where all that tension crackles and spits. You have to make the dialogue work for you no matter what emotion you're trying to evoke or what personality/voice you're hoping to portray. Here are some tips to do that.

1. KEEP DIALOGUE NATURAL AND CONSISTENT TO BOTH THE SEX OF A CHARACTER AND THEIR PERSONALITY. For instance, men often talk in monosyllables or grunts while women expound and expound and expound. A shy person might hem and haw with a lot of "ums" and "uhs," whereas a bold, pushy person will snap it out there—sure, short, and shocking. Dialogue is an opportunity to further convey a character's personality—take advantage of it! And never, *ever* use a vocabulary people wouldn't use unless it fits the character's personality.

To illustrate dialogue consistent with the SEX OF A CHARACTER: Here's a clip from *Dare to Love Again* where the hero's elderly landlady is forcing him to apologize for insulting the heroine, Alli McClare. I'm showing it two ways—example A is unnatural for the grouchy Italian police detective hero, and example B is how I actually wrote it in the book, which hopefully portrays Nicholas Barone more like the clueless male he is.

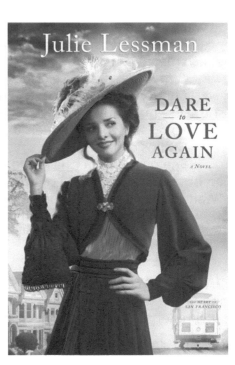

EXAMPLE A—UNNATURAL DIALOGUE

"Nicholas?" Miss Penny lifted her chin. "What do you say?"

He mauled the back of his neck. "Uh ... thank you, Miss McClare, for your gracious words, and I in turn apologize for insulting you the way I did in your classroom yesterday."

EXAMPLE B—NATURAL DIALOGUE

"Nicholas?" Miss Penny lifted her chin. "What do you say?"

He mauled the back of his neck. "Uh ... okay, I guess."

"Oh, for heaven's sake, Nicky," she said with a fold of her arms, tone stern despite a bare hint of a smile. "You say, thank you, Miss McClare, and I'm sorry for being so brash."

He swallowed the foot in his mouth, eyes on Miss McClare as he inclined his head towards Miss Penny. "Yeah, what she said."

Julie Lessman

To illustrate dialogue consistent with the PERSONALITY OF A CHARACTER: In this scene from *A Heart Revealed*, Charity O'Connor—lovingly known as a busybody in her family—is grilling the hero, Sean O'Connor (her brother), about why her best friend, Emma Malloy (the heroine), is depressed. Sean refuses to tell her anything, but Charity has her humorous ways to find out, as this scene depicts. Pay attention to the use of ellipses **(bolded)** to show dialogue where Charity is thinking out loud, almost stream of consciousness. When combined with Charity's action beats (underlined), which stress her humorous and prying personality, it not only creates a comical exchange, but also fleshes out Charity's quirkiness as a character, lending a touch of humor to lighten a pretty dark and heavy scene.

She tapped her foot on the leafy pavement. "Something's up, Sean, I can feel it in my bones, and so help me I will badger you all the way home if you don't spill it now."

His frustration blasted out in a cloud of smoke. "I can't tell you, Charity, I promised."

"Oh, fiddle, that's an easy fix. I'll just ask the questions, and you give me that stone-face look that will tell me everything I need to know."

"But that's not right."

"Sure it is," she said, dismissing his concern with a wave of her hand. "I do it with Mitch all the time." Head cocked, she chewed on her lip. **"Okay . . . it's something that happened at work, but it has to be personal because Emma's steady as a rock in all business matters, right?"**

He stared, trying not to blink.

"Okay, good, a personal situation at work that involves a person other than you."

His jaw dropped. "I never said that."

"Sure you did, when you did that pinching thing with your nose as a stall tactic."

He crossed his arms to his chest, emotional battlement to ward off the enemy.

"Now . . . let's see," she said, finger to her chin. "Somebody upset Emma pretty badly, which means it has to be someone who doesn't work at the store."

"Why?" he asked in exasperation, his patience as thin as his energy.

Charity blinked. "Why? Because the woman who bolted up my steps was as pale as death," she said, enunciating slowly as if explaining something to her nine-year-old son. "Which means it has to be someone she feels threatened by, and that rules out everyone at Dennehy's."

His lips compressed.

She gave him a quick nod and started to pace, head down and arms folded. **"Okay . . . an outsider she's afraid of and probably a man."** She halted midstride, eyes spanning wide. "Wait, it's not that bum who dated her neighbor, is it? You know, Casey's boyfriend?"

Swallowing his discomfort, he gave her a blank stare, facial muscles relaxing.

She blew out a sigh of relief. "Oh, good. For a second there, I was worried."

2. KEEP DIALOGUE NATURAL/CONSISTENT FOR THE EMOTION BEING DISPLAYED. For example, with anger, you want short, terse responses; for fear, stutters and pauses; and for flirty or teasing dialogue, make it simple, playful, and short. Of course, beats play a very important role in conveying emotion, but even beats won't work well if the dialogue doesn't match. Following is an example of a line of dialogue spoken three ways to illustrate how tone and punctuation must fit the emotion:

FEARFUL

"I ... don't believe ... you," she whispered, the blood leeching from her face.

PLAYFUL

"I'm not sure I should believe you," she said with tilt of her head, teeth tugging at the edge of her smile.

ANGRY

"I don't believe you!" he said, his voice a hiss.

In this scene from *A Passion Denied*, Marcy and Patrick O'Connor—who, by the way, have the best marriage on the planet—get in a tense fight that is almost foreign to their characters. Not only are **anger and gruff action** utilized to build the tension, but at the end of the scene, **short, bullet-fire dialogue without speaker attributions or many beats** is used to escalate it.

She was met with a cool blast of air when he snatched the covers from her body and flipped on the light. "Get up, darlin', I'd like to hear all about your evening."

Marcy sat up and put a hand to her eyes, squinting at the blinding light. "Patrick, have you been drinking?"

His laugh was not kind. "Yes, Marcy, I have. A man will often do that when he learns his wife has been unfaithful."

She pressed back against the headboard, alarmed at the brutal look in his eyes. "That's a lie! I have never been unfaithful."

"Not physically, I'm sure." His look pierced her. "At least, not until tonight."

Fear paralyzed her. "I fought him off, Patrick, I swear I did. He's a liar."

"Funny, he said the same about you."

He took a step forward, and she cowered back. Her husband had never laid a cruel hand on her. But this man was not her husband. "Patrick, you're tired, and you've been drinking. Come to bed, and we'll discuss it in the morning."

"Did you kiss him?"

"No, of course not!"

"Did he kiss you?"

She gasped for breath.

He gripped her arm and shook her. "Answer me!"

"Yes!"

His eyes glittered like ice. "Well then, Mrs. O'Connor, and how do I compare?"

3. JUST THE FACTS, MA'AM, NO FILLER. The briefest thing in our books needs to be dialogue. Let's face it—real people get irritated with real people who drone on and on about the color of something or other useless facts in a conversation. Can you imagine how your readers will feel?? Zzzzzzzzzzzzzzz!

Julie Lessman

A good rule of thumb is what my pediatrician told me long ago regarding bundling up my babies in winter. "Dress them the way you think they need to be dressed for warmth, then take half of it off." In another words—write it the way you think it needs to be said, then go in and take half of it out, distilling it down to natural listening appeal.

Example of too much filler and boring, unnecessary dialogue:

"Hey, Sue."

"Hey, Bob."

"How are you doing?" Bob said.

"Okay, I guess, and you?" Sue shifted the books in her arms, the ones she'd just purchased from the Lazy Days bookstore that her neighbor owned.

"Good, thanks." Bob buried his hands in the square pockets of his gray workpants, feeling as if he were back in grade school when he had a crush on Becky Landers, the pastor's daughter.

"It's a pretty day," Sue said.

"Yeah, it is." The lump in his throat jerked like the gumball his best friend gave him at lunch yesterday, making him wish he hadn't dropped oil on his slacks when he'd tuned up his car for his road trip next week. "I'm glad I ran into you, actually, because I was hoping I would."

"Really? Why is that?" Becky said with a shy tilt of her head, the blush on her cheeks matching the rose-colored skirt he liked, the one with buttons down the front and a short hem.

Bob smiled. "Because I was in the coffee shop for lunch and somebody put money in the jukebox to play that song that was playing when we were on that picnic in the park. You know, when we threw Frisbees and took a walk and then listened to my car radio after it started raining? All of a sudden, I was humming the song and thinking of you."

Revised dialogue—much cleaner and to the point:

"Hey, Sue—boy, am I glad I ran into you." Bob flashed a grin, heart pounding as loud as the bell in the quad tower.

She paused to shift the books in her arms with a shy tilt of her head. "Really? Why?"

He buried his hands in his pockets, sporting the same dorky smile he wore in grade school.

"'Cause the juke in the commons played *Missing You* and, well, I suddenly realized I did …"

4. UTILIZE THE POWER OF PAUSES, ELLIPSES, AND ITALICS. In these clips from *A Hope Undaunted*, Faith O'Connor learns that her husband has just hired an old girlfriend. Notice how the pauses/ellipses **(in bolded sentence)** emphasize her sister Lizzie's nervousness when she tells Faith this unwelcome news:

"Tell me what?"

Lizzie drew in a fortifying breath. "That, yes, Evelyn does have experience at Collin's father's shop because she worked there the summer before his father died." **She paused**, acid churning in her stomach. **"Which was Collin's junior year in high school … when he was …"** A lump **bobbed in Lizzie's throat. "… involved with her."**

"Involved with her?" Faith repeated, her voice barely audible.

She blinked, and Lizzie saw comprehension flicker across her sister's face, her memories of Collin's sordid past flashing through her mind, no doubt.

Faith closed her eyes. "How do you know?" she whispered.

Let's take the ellipses out of the bolded sentence and see if the effect is as strong:

She paused, acid churning in her stomach. "Which was Collin's junior year in high school when he was involved with her."

Then in the following clip, the ellipsis/italics *now* help to convey the controlled anger in Faith's question.

No one said a word as Faith quietly laid her costume aside and inched to the edge of her seat, her manner calm enough, but her voice slow and menacing. **"Well, *then* . . . is she pretty?"**

Now let's take the ellipsis and italics out of the sentence above and see if the effect is as strong:

No one said a word as Faith quietly laid her costume aside and inched to the edge of her seat, her manner calm enough, but her voice slow and menacing. "Well, then, is she pretty?"

∾

So there you have it—dialogue is very important for fleshing out your characters and creating interest and tension, romantic or otherwise. And if you don't believe me, try going out on the playground and asking if anyone would care to engage in a challenging game of streetball. The response would probably be something like, "Yo—you talkin' hoops?"

Chapter 4

Utilizing Dual Point of View

Okay, close the door and pull down the shades—we're gonna talk multiple POVs. Miss Moncado, stand guard at the door while Miss Tubbs turns up the record player to drown out what I'm about to say. To the powers that be, multiple POVs are writer's blasphemy, but Principal Mooney will back me up when I say that getting inside the heads of *both* the hero and heroine during a kiss scene intensifies desire, which in turn fires up romantic tension.

Let's face it—a kiss is something that should be explored from every angle, so if you're depicting a kiss scene from only one POV, you're missing the opportunity to double your romantic tension. Since the heroine's POV is the predominant POV in a romance novel, most kiss scenes focus on her—her feelings, her fears, her hopes for the future. But when you flesh out the scene with the hero's POV as well, you can show his strength, his gentleness, his dominance, or even his angst at falling in love with a woman he wants but can't have. *Ahem* … like Rhett with Scarlett in *Gone with the Wind* or … Collin with Faith in *A Passion Most Pure*.

A WORD OF WARNING: Some publishers frown on more than one POV in a scene because they believe it's too confusing. I, on the other hand, think it hikes the tension and sigh factor when you incorporate both. However, you MUST follow some basic rules if you plan to switch POVs mid-scene:

1. Always double-space to indicate a change of POV, or as Revell allows me to do in my novels, insert a dash between POVs.
2. Always begin the new POV with an action by the new-POV character.
3. Keep POV switches to a minimum per scene and always flesh out each POV with several paragraphs/pages (NEVER switch POVs every sentence/paragraph).

Here is a scene from *A Hope Undaunted* that looks at a first kiss through the eyes of the hero Luke McGee via his POV utilizing both internal monologue (Luke's thoughts) and dialogue. At a crucial point in the scene, we then flip to the POV of the heroine, Katie O'Connor, for her reaction, upping the tension ante considerably.

He plunged his hands in his pockets and softened his tone. "Katie … is it me? Did I say or do something to upset you?"

She shook her head, gaze bonded to the floor. "No, Luke, really, please, I just need to—"

He nudged her chin up with his thumb, and her lips parted with a sharp intake of breath. And then he saw it. The gentle rise and fall of her chest, the soft rose in her cheeks, the skittish look in her eyes, flitting to his lips and then quickly away. Comprehension suddenly oozed through him like heated honey purling through his veins. Could it be? Was it possible that cold, callous Katie O'Connor was beginning to warm up? To him, of all people—the leper from her past? The thought sent warm ripples of shock through his body, thinning the air in his lungs. His gaze gentled, taking in the vulnerability in her eyes, the fear in her face, and all he wanted to do was hold her, reassure her.

Julie Lessman

As if under a spell, his gaze was drawn to her lips, parted and full, and the sound of her shallow breathing filled him with a fierce longing. "Oh, Katie," he whispered, no power over the pull he was suddenly feeling. In slow motion, he bent toward her, closing his eyes to caress her mouth with his own. A weak gasp escaped her as she stiffened, but he couldn't relent. The taste of her lips was far more than he bargained for, and he drew her close with a raspy groan. With a fierce hold, he cupped the back of her neck and kissed her deeply, gently, possessive in his touch. His fingers twined in her hair, desperate to explore.

And then all at once, beyond his comprehension, her body melded to his with an answering groan, and he was shocked when her mouth rivaled his with equal demand. Desire licked through him, searing his body and then his conscience. With a heated shudder, he gripped her arms and pushed her back, his breathing ragged as he held her at bay. "We can't do this," he whispered. He dropped his hold and exhaled, gouging shaky fingers through disheveled hair. His gaze returned, capturing hers and riddled with regret. "Believe me, Katie, as much as I want to, I've learned the hard way to take things slow. I should have never started this, and I'm sorry. Will you forgive me?"

—

Forgive him? She stared at him through glazed eyes, her pulse still pumping in her veins at a ridiculous rate. She never wanted this, couldn't stand the sight of him, and now here she was, tingling from his touch and desperate for more. Addicted to the "King of Misery." The very thought inflamed both fury and desire at the same time, muddling her mind. Dear Lord, she was torn between welding her lips to his or slapping him silly. With a tight press of her mouth, she opted for the second and smacked him clean across the face.

Now imagine the scene above *without* Katie's POV where you lose the benefit of her thoughts. She would come off hard and a little crazy, returning his kiss with passion one moment and then slapping him silly the next. But the double POV—being privy to her frustration over her unwelcome attraction to the bane of her existence *and* seeing Luke's attraction to her through his eyes—heightens the tension, not only for this scene, but for all the scenes ahead.

❧

In summation, you might say Double POV is a wee bit like Doublemint gum, although I am certainly not a proponent of gum in the classroom. But I will admit that with Double POV, a little bit of his or her thoughts goes a long way to "double your pleasure, double your fun."

WHACK! Miss Herringshaw—spit that gum out right now, young lady, and throw it in the trash!

Chapter 5

Escalating Romantic Tension with Anger

KA-BANG! Despite this stick in my hand, I am *not* a violent person, but anger has to be one of my *favorite* ways to up the romantic tension in a story. So much so that I'm known as a "CDQ" (caffeinated drama queen) who likes lots of angst and drama in my novels. The way I figure it, it's better to channel all that churning drama into my books instead of my marriage, which is a good thing for my hubby, yes, but not so good for my characters!

In my ebook release, *A Light in the Window: An Irish Love Story*, the hero and heroine's first kiss in the clip below is prompted by the heroine's rejection and the hero's subsequent anger. Not only does "anger" immediately set up the romantic tension between these two right off the bat, but it sets the tone for the rest of the book where the Southie heartthrob is forced to slowly change his ways to win the heart of the woman who despises him. And, yes, that's my daughter on the cover that my hubby designed. Great job, eh?

Seconds passed like eons before she finally shook her head. "I'm sorry, Patrick, really I am. I like you as a person, truly, but in the romantic sense, I have no desire to be involved with a man like you, a rogue who so casually equates lust with love."

A man like you.

A failure. A sinner. Someone not worthy of love. To his parents, and now, apparently, to Marceline Murphy. Her pious judgment detonated his temper. Fists clenched, he leaned in, eyes itching hot. "So you're judge and jury then, are you, Marceline? Condemning me without knowing me?"

Her jaw notched up, his tone apparently sparking her anger as well. "I may not know *you*, Mr. O'Connor, but I *do* know this neighborhood is littered with broken hearts and tarnished reputations at your hand. So if you'll kindly unhand my portfolio, you can be on your way."

She might as well have spit in his face. He stood paralyzed except for the white-hot fury that scorched through him, stunned at her blatant rejection. Once again, Christian piety at its very best—judging him, condemning him, telling him he would never measure up. Deemed imperfect by imperfect people.

The leather portfolio burned in his palm like the angst burned in his gut, and he could hardly fathom that the one woman he longed to know condemned him just like his father. The very notion caused the blood to pound in his brain, and his response was swift, defiant, and rash. "Yes, I'll unhand your portfolio, Miss Murphy," he said with a strained whisper, fingers taut as they fisted the leather. "But first ... you revile me as a rogue? I'll give you a rogue ..."

He hurled the attaché to the ground and jerked her close, temple throbbing as he silenced her with his mouth. Stilling the lash of her arms with a dominant hold, he took his fill of a beauty who had cut him to the core, wounded his pride, and spurned him as cruelly as his own blood.

The stolen kiss of a rogue—just punishment for a woman who had stolen his heart, crushing it beneath the heel of faith in a so-called loving God.

His trigger reaction had been prompted by revenge, making her pay, but she tasted of roses and peppermint and a summer so warm, his anger flamed into desire, filling him with a savage possession. Palm braced to the back of her neck, he devoured her with a low groan, totally undone by the woman in his arms. "Marceline," he rasped, voice hoarse as he cupped her face in his hands. "This is not how I meant it to be . . ."

Chest heaving, she lurched away, the stinging jolt of her slap vibrating his jaw till his teeth rattled in his skull. "How dare you!"

He blinked, the strike of her anger diffusing his own and breaking the spell the kiss had cast. "How dare I?" he whispered. A gloom darker than the blackest of nights crawled into his soul. "How dare I do anything else, Marceline, but be all you've proclaimed me to be?"

&#x3;␷

In the following scene from *A Hope Undaunted*, the hero, Luke McGee, walks away from a friendship with the heroine, Katie O'Connor (whose POV we are in), because although he's in love with her, she plans to marry her boyfriend Jack. In the beginning of this clip, Luke's heartbreak is evident, but notice the tension that pops at the very end when Luke's anger is introduced.

"Wait!" She ran to grasp his arm in a death hold, fingers clenched as tight as her stomach. "Don't do this, please—don't just walk away. I care about you, Luke, and I need your friendship. And you need mine."

His gaze fixed on her hand where Jack's diamond glittered in the lamplight, then slowly rose to her face, his blue eyes almost black. "No, Katie," he whispered with a thread of pain in his voice, "I need your love."

Her heart crashed to a stop. She removed her hand and lowered her eyes, her gaze fused to the fringed tongue of his brown leather shoe. "I . . . care about you, Luke, I do." Her voice trailed off, fragile and reedy with regret. "But please . . . why can't we just be friends?"

Taut fingers gripped her chin and jerked it up, the dominance of his hold matched by the anger in his eyes. "Because it will be lovers or nothing, Katie Rose. The choice is yours."

&#x3;␷

Oh, sweet summer vacation, if there's a faster way to inject romantic tension into a book than anger, I sure don't know what it is. And if you do—I want a term paper on it by tomorrow, and I'll guarantee an A!

Chapter 6

Using All Five Senses for Heightened Effect

All right boys and girls, just as our school cafeteria is a feast for the stomach, romance is a feast for the senses. Although it's been many, *many* years since I was in school, I'm not so ancient that I can't remember the sights, sounds, smells, and taste of one of my very first kisses. A young boy had plucked a handful of lilacs for me—my favorite flower—in the rain, no less, and to this day, I can still smell that heavenly scent. Still feel that cool wetness of water droplets on my hand as I held that rain-kissed bouquet. Still hear the patter of raindrops on my porch roof mingled with my own soft breathing as his lips gently brushed mine, the taste of peppermint teasing my senses.

Ahem . . . but I digress. Romance is clearly a sensory thing in which touch, taste, seeing, hearing, and smelling play a crucial part, not only for the hero and heroine, but for the reader as well, so try to incorporate as many senses as possible. Three senses are a must and five, although difficult to do, hits the sensory jackpot!

Here's a clip from *Love at Any Cost* in which I think the five senses **(all bolded)** play an important role in allowing the reader to see, hear, smell, taste, and feel/touch the scene along with the characters.

His heart seized when **she pressed a kiss to his cheek [touch]**, and almost by accident, **he turned into her silky caress [touch]**, their lips so close he could **smell the hint of hot chocolate [smell]** they'd enjoyed around the fire. They froze in the same split second of time, and his pulse thudded slow and hard as he waited for her to pull away. Only she didn't, and heat scorched his body when **her shallow breathing warmed his skin [hear and touch]**.

"Cait," he whispered, barely believing her lips nearly grazed his. **All he could hear was the roar of blood in his ears [hear]** as he waited, not willing to push for fear she would retreat, **but when her eyelids flickered closed [sight]**, his fate was sealed. "So help me, Cait, I love you," he rasped, **nuzzling her lips [touch]** before she could retreat. **The moment his mouth took hers [touch],** he was a man hopelessly lost, bewitched by her spell.

She jolted in his arms [touch] as if suddenly realizing her folly, but he refused to relent, **his grip at the nape of her neck strong and sure [touch]. A delicious dizziness overtook him at the taste of the sweetest lips he'd ever known, a heady tease of chocolate and peppermint and Caitlyn McClare [taste].** A groan trapped in his throat, and he devoured her, delving deeper with a passion stoked by almost twenty-six years of denial and longing. "God help me, Cait," he whispered, voice hoarse as he feathered her ear. "I need you in my life."

❧❦

Now, let's give you a chance to decide for yourself which you prefer—a clip with sensory components or without. Here's a scene from *A Light in the Window* presented both ways—with all senses in play and without.

EXAMPLE WITH FEW SENSES IN PLAY

He rested his head on the back of his chair with a loose fold of arms, watching her through lidded eyes while his pulse thumped slow and sure. A breeze feathered the tendrils of her hair against an alabaster neck, teasing both Patrick and the delicate lobe of her ear. He imagined suckling that very ear and his throat parched dry, compelling him to bolt another swig of milk.

He forced himself to focus on the person rather than the woman, and a calm settled like nothing he had ever experienced before. There was a reserved innocence that intrigued him and a gentle depth that called, both to his body and his soul. And although he didn't know much about the grown-up Marceline Murphy, he did know one thing for dead sure. This was a woman he wanted to know better—and in every possible way.

EXAMPLE WITH ALL SENSES IN PLAY

He rested his head on the back of his chair with a loose fold of arms, watching her through lidded eyes while his pulse thumped slow and sure. **He was mesmerized by the pale gold that tumbled her shoulders, transfixed by the soft shape of her mouth, the silk of her skin [sight].** A honeysuckle breeze feathered his face [smell and touch]** as well as the tendrils of hair against her alabaster neck, teasing both Patrick and the delicate lobe of her ear. **He imagined suckling that very ear [touch]** and his throat parched dry, **compelling him to bolt another swig of milk. It suddenly tasted as sour as Marcy's opinion of rogues like him [taste],** and he swallowed hard.

Forcing himself to focus on the person rather than the woman, he felt a calm settle like nothing he'd ever experienced before, as soft and soothing **as the scent of roses she wore [smell].** There was a reserved innocence that intrigued him and a gentle depth that called, both to his body and his soul. And although he didn't know much about the grown-up Marceline Murphy, he did know one thing for dead sure. This was a woman he wanted to know better— and in every possible way.

❧❦

Now, I don't know about you, but as a teacher in a classroom, I prefer to have ALL my senses in play so I can **see** and **smell** when students are chewing gum before I whack the desk with a loud crack (**touch and hear**). Of course, **taste** comes in when I confiscate the gum like I did with Miss Dawn Crandall, who will have extra homework tonight writing, "I will not chew gum in Mrs. Lessman's class" 100 times on loose-leaf paper.

Chapter 7

Cashing in on the Kid and Pet Factor

Dogs, cats, kids, babies—doesn't matter—put one in the arms of a good-looking hero, and you have instant attraction for most women. Put a kiss in the middle of that hero, dog, cat, kid, or baby and *look out*—you've got yourself a tender kiss that can warm the page with romantic innocence so sweet, it will illicit a sigh.

Hopefully I succeeded in doing that in this scene from *A Love Surrendered,* where Glory, the heroine's five-year-old sister, has *just* given the hero a sweet peck on the lips after he drove her and her sister Annie home.

"G'night, Glory." He tapped her nose before Annie managed to pry her away.

"Thanks again," Annie said, inching through the door with Glory in her arms.

"Wait! Aren't you going to kiss her too?" Glory spun around, eyes wide with the innocence of a little girl who had no earthly idea what she was asking him to do.

He blinked, noting the expanse of Annie's eyes.

"Glory, no—" she whispered, turning ten kinds of pale.

"Please?" The little troublemaker stared at him with those wide eyes of an angel.

Heart thudding, he did the only thing he knew to do—he kissed Annie right on the tip of her nose. Clearing his throat, he stepped back. "Well, good-night, ladies."

"No, silly," Glory said, "like this . . ." She demonstrated with a sweet little peck on her sister's lips as if he were too stupid to understand, then tilted her head. "See? It's easy."

Too easy, he thought with a trip of his pulse. *Way, way too easy . . .*

"Stop it, Glory, Steven doesn't want to—"

"Sure I do," he whispered, his words shocking him as much as Annie. Gaze holding hers, he slowly leaned in, close enough to see the long sweep of her lashes, the pale gold in eyes so green, he felt like he was in Oz, about to be granted a wish. He heard the soft hitch of her breath when she stopped breathing because it coincided with the halt of air in his own lungs. Cupping her face in his hand, his eyelids sheathed closed at the touch of her lips—soft, supple and just a hint of peppermint from the candy she'd offered him in the car. It was meant to be no more than a peck like Glory had given him, but somehow his mouth wanted to linger and explore . . . He stepped in close, body grazing hers and Glory's till they were one. A little-girl giggle broke the trance, and Annie's lips curved beneath his.

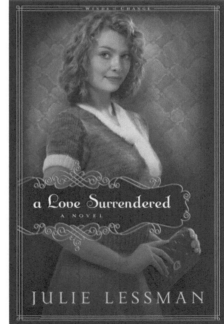

"His whiskers are itchy, aren't they, Annie?" Glory asked, patting his face once again. "Kinda makes you wiggly all over, doesn't it?"

Annie's eyes glowed as she caressed her own cheek. "Very wiggly," she whispered.

❧❧

And let's not leave the pets out! Here's another scene from *A Love Surrendered,* where a subordinate heroine conspires with her cats against her husband. Go ahead—tell me the pets don't ramp up the romantic tension in *this* scene …

Kicking off her shoes, Emma spanned across the covers on her tummy, kneading Lancelot's paw while she stroked Guinevere's head, her mind straying to how much her life had changed since Sean had made her his wife. In him she had everything she'd ever hoped for in a marriage.

Except for his children, she reminded herself, and the thought prompted her to close her eyes and pray until she heard the bathroom door open. The bed vibrated with the purrs of her former bedmates, bringing a giggle to her lips. "So, how was your evening, your highness and your majesty?" she said with a soft scrub of their fur. "I know you're not pleased my husband steals your snuggle time, but remember, once he closes his eyes, he's gone for the night, so just bide your time …"

"Are you conspiring with those cats again, Emma O'Connor?" Sean assessed her with a shuttered gaze, arms folded and hip cocked in the doorway. Sculpted chest bare, he ambled into the room in boxers and blond hair damp from his shower. A slow grin of warning stretched across wide lips as he eased onto the bed to lie beside her. Elbow cocked and head in hand, he massaged Guinevere's ribcage, warming Emma with a dangerous smile. Leaning close, he grazed her lips, then pulled away, the blue eyes tripping her pulse. "You're next," he whispered.

❧❧

Okay, that's class for today, and remember, students—sometimes it's okay for your writing to go to the dogs, especially when a love scene is involved!

Chapter 8

Enhancing Mood with Emotionally Charged Words/Verbs

Question: If somebody spread a nasty rumor about you at school, would you be "mad" or would you be "seething with fury"?

When the recess bell rings, do you "walk" outside to the playground or do you "bolt"?

If the cafeteria serves your favorite dessert—warm peach cobbler with ice cream—do you "eat" it or do you "devour" it?

Pull or *jerk*, *push* or *thrust*—the words you choose DO make a difference in the tension level of a scene *and* in the emotional response you hope to elicit from the reader.

In the following paragraph from *A Hope Undaunted,* the hero, Luke McGee, loses his temper when the heroine, Katie O'Connor, responds to his innocent kiss with heated passion, then hauls off and whacks him, blasting him with a verbal insult to boot. Luke's fury manifests itself in dominance, so notice the use of emotionally charged words such as *devour, consume, guttural, ravage,* all bolded below. Each further enhances the drama of an already tense situation, ratching up the romantic tension.

She tried to **shove** him out of the way. "I'm going home."

"Not yet," he whispered, **blocking** her in with a **push** to the wall ...

In a catch of her breath, he **took** her mouth **by force**, his late-day beard **rough** against her skin. A faint moan escaped her lips and all **resistance** fled, **burned** away by the heat of his touch, leaving her weak and wanting. His mouth roamed at will, no longer gentle as he **devoured** her, **ravenous** against the smooth curve of her throat, the soft flesh of her ear. With a **guttural** groan, he **jerked** her close with **powerful** arms, **consuming** her mouth with a kiss surely **driven** by the **sheer will** to **ravage**.

❧

Likewise, in the following paragraph from *A Passion Denied*, Marcy O'Connor's mood over her husband's rejection is paralleled with both the dismal weather and death, increasing the romantic tension in this usually strong marriage that's been torn apart by a horrendous fight. Note the use of words like *bleak, slithered, endless weeping, gray and dismal, grief, loss, silent mourning, cold and dead, corpse,* which hopefully set the mood and raise the tension. Whenever possible you want to correlate words with something else to help drive the point home and make the tension even more taut.

Marcy stood at Mrs. Gerson's kitchen window, in **bleak** harmony with the rivulets of water that **slithered** down the pane. It was a **slow and steady rain**, **endless weeping** from a **gray and dismal sky**, and Marcy felt a kinship with it. It showed no signs of letting up, much like the

Julie Lessman

grief in her heart over the **loss** of her husband. A **silent mourning** over a spouse who was still very much alive, but whose love was as **cold and dead** as any **corpse**.

In the following clip from *A Passion Redeemed,* the hero, Mitch Dennehy, is irate over his attraction to the heroine, Charity O'Connor, the woman he wants nothing to do with because she ruined his life. Note how his anger is manifested and magnified by words such as *hurled, bludgeoned, growled,* or *vicious,* volatile verbs/words that reflect his mood and ratchet the romantic tension.

He reached in his jacket and **hurled** a wad of bills on the bar. "To the devil with my future. It might as well **fry** with the past."

He **wheeled around** and **bludgeoned** his way through the crowd, **riling** customers on his way out. Outside, the **bitter** cold **assailed** him, tinged with the smells of burning peat and the slight whiff of horses. He could hear the faint sound of laughter and singing drifting from the various pubs tucked along the cobblestone road. His **anger swelled**.

He **flung** his car door open and **chucked** the bottle on the passenger seat. Mumbling under his breath, he rounded the vehicle to rotate the crank, **gyrating** the lever with such **ferocity** that it **rattled unmercifully**. The engine **growled** to life, its **vicious roar** rivaling the **angst** in his gut. He got in the car and **slammed** the door, **slapping** the headlights on with a **grunt**. With a **hard swipe** of the steering wheel, he **jerked** the car away from the curve and exhaled a loud breath.

It was happening again. He was finally past the pain of one sister and now it was beginning with the other. He **gunned** the vehicle down Lower Abbey Street, nearly **bashing** a pedestrian who probably wouldn't have felt a thing, given the near-empty bottle in his hand. Mitch **gritted** his teeth. That's what women did to you—drove you to the bottom of a bottle where you drowned in your own liquid **travail**. He **yanked** his tie off, loosening his shirt to let the **frigid** air cool the heat of his anger. Thoughts of Charity suddenly surfaced, and a heat of another kind **surged** through his body. He swore out loud, the **coarse** sound foreign to his ears. He turned the corner on a **squeal**. The bottle **careened** across the seat and **slammed** into his leg.

He'd been without a woman way too long. Once, his appetite had been **voracious**. But Faith had changed all that. Her sincerity, her purity, her honesty. She had **ruined** him for other women. Since she'd left, he'd had no inclination, no interest. No desire.

Until now.

Now I ask you—take a look at each of these sentences from the clip above and tell me which you prefer to convey the appropriate anger in this scene, A or B?

A) He turned and made his way through the crowd, disturbing customers on his way out.

OR

B) He wheeled around and bludgeoned his way through the crowd, riling customers on his way out.

22

A) He opened his car door and threw the bottle on the passenger seat. Mumbling under his breath, he rounded the vehicle to rotate the crank, turning the lever till it shook.

OR

B) He flung his car door open and chucked the bottle on the passenger seat. Mumbling under his breath, he rounded the vehicle to rotate the crank, gyrating the lever with such ferocity that it rattled unmercifully.

❧❧

A) The engine came to life, its rumbling rivaling the upset in his gut. He got in the car and closed the door, turning the headlights on. With a swivel of the steering wheel, he pulled the car away from the curve and exhaled a loud breath.

OR

B) The engine growled to life, its vicious roar rivaling the angst in his gut. He got in the car and slammed the door, slapping the headlights on with a grunt. With a hard swipe of the steering wheel, he jerked the car away from the curve and exhaled a loud breath.

❧❧

Okay, class—pass your papers to the front! Test grades will be distributed tomorrow and some of you will be happy (**ecstatic**), no doubt, dancing (**gyrating**) in the streets, and others will be sad (**devastated**), crying (**sobbing**) into your milk. Your choice, your mood.

LISTEN UP, PEOPLE—MAJOR TIP FOR POWER WORDS! What I am about to give you is worth the price of this book and more, so put this link on your "favorites."

The **BEST** online thesaurus I have *ever* come across is the **OneLook Reverse Dictionary**, a website I keep open constantly when I write. Here's the link, and you're welcome! http://onelook.com/reverse-dictionary.shtml.

Chapter 9

Capitalizing on the Element of Surprise

Surprise is always fun, but never more so than in a scene where "attraction" is underscored despite neither party expecting it. It's fun to shock a hero or heroine with feelings they don't expect, because let's face it, catching a guy (or a gal) off-guard with a kiss or attraction provides top-notch romantic tension.

Here is an example of attraction sneaking up on both the hero and heroine in an unlikely situation from *A Passion Redeemed*. Mitch Dennehy has no problem being in control until Charity O'Connor gets a *little* too close for comfort. The surprise of attraction once again reminds the hero—and the reader—that romantic tension is alive and well in this story.

He grabbed her wrist. "Where are you going? It's late. You need to wait for a ride."

She yanked her arm free and seared him with a look that grieved him to the core, wrapping her coat loosely over her shoulders. "No thanks. I'd rather walk."

He leapt up and pushed her back in the booth. "You're not walking anywhere. You'll wait till I'm good and ready to take you home."

She jumped back up, hair flying wild and nostrils flaring. "I hate you!" she cried, lashing at him with her nails. He clutched her wrists. She started kicking and flailing, her protest drawing attention. His blood began to boil. With a grunt, he locked her in a vise and bent his mouth hard against her ear. "So help me, Charity, the more you fight, the more it'll hurt."

"Let me go," she hissed, her breath coming hard.

"Are you going to behave?"

She didn't answer.

He tightened his grip, feeling the pounding of her heart as he locked her against his chest.

"Yes, you overgrown ape."

He fought a grin. "Promise. Although we both know your promises aren't worth the air that surrounds them, I'm willing to give you one more chance. Promise you'll settle down and wait for me to take you home."

He felt her resistance fade as she slowly relaxed against his chest. "I promise."

He softened his hold. All at once, he was painfully aware of every curve of her body, pressed hard against his. Heat infused him, shooting up the back of his neck and into his face. He flung her away, pushing her into the booth as if his fingers burned at her touch.

She looked up, almost prone on the seat, hair and coat splayed behind her. The deep V of that amazing blouse rose and fell with every hard breath she took. The slightest tilt of a smile shadowed her lips as she arched a perfectly shaped brow. "Why Mr. Dennehy, I do believe you're blushing."

❧❧

I actually incorporated the element of surprise into the very first love scene I ever wrote in my debut novel, *A Passion Most Pure*. The rogue hero, Collin McGuire, takes heroine Faith O'Connor by surprise with a kiss in the park after Faith warns him to stay away from her sister. The surprise, however, is actually on Collin when he discovers a powerful attraction to Faith that scares him silly.

She shot off the blanket and glared down at him, elbows flaring at her side. "You leave her alone! She's not one of your common girls at Brannigan's. She's a good girl. Too good for the likes of you."

"*Too good for the likes of you . . .*" His mother's words assaulted his memory, flaming the fuse. Springing to his feet, he towered over Faith and gripped her shoulders, fingers digging in. For an instant, it appeared as if she didn't dare breathe.

"Don't ever say that again," he whispered, his jaw hard as rock. Fury pulsed in his temple. He tightened his grip. "Too good for the likes of me, is she now? Well then, what about you, Faith O'Connor? Are you too good for the likes of me?"

She caught her breath just before his lips found hers, and he felt the fight within her as he locked her in his arms. The taste of her mouth was so heady to his senses, a soft moan escaped his lips at the shock of it. She shivered before she went weak in his arms, and instinctively, he softened his hold.

Her lunge took him by surprise when she clipped the edge of his jaw with a tight-fisted punch, her breath coming in ragged gasps. "How dare you—" she sputtered, the green eyes full of heat.

He grinned and silenced her with his mouth. She made a weak attempt to push him away, but he only drew her back with a force that made her shudder. He felt her pulse racing as his lips wandered her throat. The scent of her drove him mad. He kissed her with renewed urgency, the taste of her making him dizzy. And then, before she could catch her breath, he shoved her away, his heart thundering and his mind paralyzed.

❧❧

Surprise! You'll have to read the rest in the book.

POP! Miss Casey Herringshaw, take that slimy toad outside this moment. Surprise is fine in romance, but *not* in my classroom!

Chapter 10

Exposing Desire in an Unwilling Character

KA-POW! Miss Stiehr—I don't care if your father is superintendent or not, you will put that cell phone away this instant.

All right, students—shoulders straight, eyes on the board. Today we are going to expose desire in an unwilling character. Like Miss Stiehr's infraction upped the tension in my classroom just now, few things can up the tension in a book like revealing an unwilling attraction in a hero. There is something so emotionally charged about a person whose romantic vulnerabilities are exposed (i.e., the concept of still waters running deep—think Mr. Darcy in *Pride & Prejudice* or Ashley Wilkes in *Gone with the Wind*). Dormant desire is a human condition we all relate to and when it's brought to the surface, sparks can fly.

Here is a scene from *A Passion Denied*, where the hero, John Brady, is attracted to the heroine, Lizzie O'Connor (whom he calls "Beth"), but refuses to admit it because he sees her only as a little sister and good friend. But Lizzie has other ideas and implements a "plot" devised by her sister, Charity, to breach Brady's defenses with a kiss.

When Lizzie remembers Charity's words that "a kiss is the only thing that will haunt him until he admits he's in love" she engages the "plot" to take him by surprise. Suddenly the tension in this scene is stretched as taut as a quivering rubber band, guaranteeing a clean shot with a definite sting.

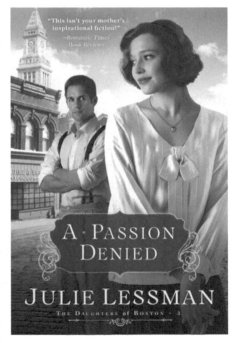

"Beth, don't cry, please. I love you …"

She felt his lips in her hair, and her anguish soared. She jerked away. "No, don't lie to me, Brady! You don't love me—"

He groaned and embraced her. "I do love you, little buddy, more than anyone in this world." With grief in his eyes, he studied her swollen face, caressing her wet cheeks with gentle hands. "You mean everything to me," he whispered. He bent to press a light kiss to her forehead.

Shallow breaths rose from her throat at the warmth of his lips against her skin. Her body stilled. *"A kiss is the only thing that will haunt him until he admits he's in love."*

She lifted her gaze, taking great care to impart a slow sweep of lashes.

"Beth, are we okay?" He ducked his head to search her eyes, then brushed her hair back from her face. A smile shadowed his lips. "Still friends?"

Friends. A deadly plague only a kiss could cure. Resolve stiffened her spine. "Sure, Brady … friends."

He smiled and tucked a finger under her chin. "That's my girl. Now what do you say we pray about some of these things?" He leaned close with another quick kiss to her brow, and in a desperate beat of her heart, she lunged, uniting her mouth with his. She felt the shock of her action in the jolt of his body, and she gripped him close to deepen the kiss. Waves of warmth shuddered through her at the taste of him, and the essence of peppermint was sweet in her mouth.

"No!" He wrenched back from her hold with disbelief in his eyes.

Julie Lessman

Too late. She had never felt like this before. Years of seeking romance from flat parchment pages had not prepared her for this. This rush, this desire … her body suddenly alive, and every nerve pulsing with need. All shyness melted away in the heat of her longing, and she pounced again, merging her mouth with his. *John Brady, I love you!*

A fraction of a second became eons as she awaited his rejection. His body was stiff with shock, but no resistance came. And in a sharp catch of her breath, he drew her to him with such force, she gasped, the sound silenced by the weight of his mouth against hers. He groaned and cupped the back of her head as if to delve in her soul, a man possessed. His lips broke free to wander her throat, and shivers of heat coursed through her veins. In ragged harmony, their shallow breathing billowed into the night while his arms possessed her, molding her body to his.

"Oh, Brady, I'm so in love with you," she whispered.

Her words severed his hold as neatly as the blade of a guillotine. He staggered to his feet, and icy cold replaced the warmth of his arms.

❧⚜❧

There's no question that I am a bona fide CDQ because I love taking people—especially characters and readers—by surprise. In the following scene from *A Passion Redeemed*, heroine Charity O'Connor—a master plotter in affairs of the heart—surprises the hero, Mitch Dennehy, first by hiding in the backseat of his car, then by stealing a kiss.

She stared in disbelief, the fire in her eyes burning away any good intent. He wouldn't even hear her out? Give her five minutes of his time? After all they'd been to each other? She groaned and pounced, pummeling his arm as hard as she could. "You can go to the devil, Mitch Dennehy, for all I care, but first we're going to talk."

He shoved her back on the seat. "Get out of my car, *now*."

She propped up on her elbows, her jaw quivering with anger. "Make me."

He lunged to open her door, and she battered his chest while tears blurred in her eyes. Straddling her to deflect her blows, he forced her wrists to the seat, breathing hard as she fought. A choked sob broke from her lips, and the anger faded from his face.

And then she saw it. Pain, regret, longing. Her conscience stilled and her pulse picked up. As if against her will, her own longing took control.

He loves me still!

He loosened his hold and backed away. His tone was pleading. "Charity, please do us both a favor and go home."

Hope surged and she grabbed his shirt, wrenching him down until their lips met. He groaned and finished the job, devouring her mouth with his own. She moaned softly and pressed in, clutching him with all her might. "You love me, I knew it!"

He launched back to his side of the car, his breathing out of control. "So … help … me, I will hurt you if you come at me again."

❧⚜❧

In romance, if there's attraction between two characters, "unwillingness" on the part of one of the parties only stirs the romantic pot, so don't be afraid to turn up the heat.

Chapter 11

Immediate Hero/Heroine Confrontation

Ah, confrontation—undesirable in a classroom, yes, but in a novel? Oh, honey, it spikes tension better than a cast-iron ruler slapping a wooden desk—***CRR-AAA-CKKK!***

You might **say** immediate confrontation is the perfect volley in a fast-paced game of the wills, in which disdain, sarcasm, withering looks, or insults set the hero and heroine up in a head-butting match that's sure to end in a game of love.

Here's an **example** from *A Passion Most Pure* where the sweet and gentle heroine, Faith O'Connor, first meets her new boss, Mitch Dennehy, with whom she eventually falls in love. Mitch is a handsome but cantankerous newspaper editor who does not want her on his staff, and Faith O'Connor is a redhead with an Irish temper she usually keeps under wraps. After Mitch is 45 minutes late for a meeting, his boss Michael (in whose POV we are in) introduces the two, resulting in Mitch badgering Faith with snide questions. She responds with polite but cool answers ... *until* she ends the confrontation with a well-placed zinger.

Michael turned to Faith. "Faith, this ... ," he said with a touch of drama, "is your manager, Mitch Dennehy."

Faith turned in her seat to acknowledge Mitch, whose frosty gaze shifted from her face, down to her new, leather shoes and back up again. His blue eyes assessed her so completely, her cheeks bruised crimson as she stiffened in the chair, chin thrust high. "Hello, Mr. Dennehy," she said, her tone polite but cool.

Mitch didn't say a word, only eyed her with practiced superiority, and the blush on her cheeks spread like blight in the rainy season. Michael watched in fascination as a smile fluttered on his department editor's lips.

Mitch's penetrating blue eyes drifted from the tiny hands pinched white in Faith's lap, to the soft tendril of hair that curved the nape of her neck. "Michael tells me you were a copywriter at *The Boston Herald*, is that right?"

Faith hesitated, then sucked in a shaky breath. "Yes, I mean I did write some copy ..."

Mitch nodded. His cocky smile worked its way into a grin. "Some copy? Have you done any feature writing before?" He was waiting. They were all waiting.

The hot stain on her cheeks was a permanent condition now. "No, I haven't done much feature writing, exactly ..."

"Any reviews, editorials, hard news?"

She tensed as if straddling a mule about to buck. "No, I'm afraid I don't have much experience doing any of that ..."

"Well, then, Miss O'Connor," he mused, his eyes laughing at her, "tell me. Is there anything you can do?"

The air stilled to a deathly hush. Slowly, she lifted her chin to stare at him with as much defiance as she could politely display. "Yes sir ... ," she said, producing a smile that was anything but. "I can be on time."

In my second book in the Heart of San Francisco series, *Dare to Love Again*, the first half of the book is chock-full of glorious confrontation between the hero and heroine. It should be no secret to my readers that I absolutely adore the male-vs.-female head-butting confrontations you see in the old John Wayne/Maureen O'Hara movies like *McClintock*. In fact, I had *so* much fun writing immediate hero/heroine confrontation in *A Passion Redeemed* and *A Hope Undaunted* that I wanted to try it again in *Dare to Love Again*. Here's a clip from the opening of that book where sarcasm (and eventually flailing sticks) set up the ultimate love confrontation. I even utilized an ongoing "caveman" theme **(bolded)** through the first half of the book, which hopefully lends humor as well as romantic tension.

Merciful Providence ... I smell a rat! Allison McClare sniffed, eyes in a squint and nose in the air, the unmistakable scent of Bay Rum drifting in her empty classroom at the Hand of Hope School. Although not uncommon for an antiquated Victorian house a stone's throw from the sewers of the Barbary Coast, *this* smell of "rat" was altogether different and far more frightening. She wrinkled her nose.

The man kind.

"I think you took a wrong turn, lady. High tea is at The Palace."

"Oh!" Body jolting, she whirled around at the bulletin board, almost inhaling the straight pin in her teeth. She blinked at a tall, disgruntled stranger cocked in the door of her classroom, who might have been dangerously attractive if not for the scowl on his face. An unruly strand of dark hair, almost black—like his mood appeared to be—toppled over his forehead beneath a dark Homburg he obviously felt no courtesy to remove.

He hiked a thumb toward the front door, his gruff voice a near snarl as he glared through gray-green eyes that seemed to darken by the moment, the color of stormy seas. "I assume that's your fancy car and driver out front? Well it needs to move to the back alley, lady, whether you're here to teach or just out slumming with the poor folks."

The straight pin in her teeth dropped to the floor along with her jaw. She gaped, hardly able to comprehend the rudeness of this **Neanderthal** who'd be better attired in **bearskin and club** than the charcoal suit coat draped over his shoulder. Rolled sleeves of what might have been a crisp white shirt at one time revealed muscled **forearms thick with dark hair** like the **brainless caveman** he appeared to be. It was only two in the afternoon, but already **dark bristle** shadowed his **hard-angled jaw**, lending an ominous air to a man who possessed less charm than found on the head of her pin.

And a head just as pointed.

Her nose scrunched, the smell of "rat" surprisingly strong due to a keen sense of smell and three near-misses at the altar. She fought the squirm of a smile as she took in his high starched collar and off-center four-in-hand tie—loosened as if in protest to fashionable attire he considered a noose 'round his neck.

Like the one I'm envisioning right now ...

He squinted as if she were the intruder instead of him, daring to invade his **cave**. "What, cat got your tongue?"

Yes, you pinhead ... a polecat. She glared right back in silence, figuring if she waited long enough, his face would crack ... something she'd pay good money to see. She almost wished she'd gone home with Mother and Cassie earlier instead of attempting to stay later on a Friday the week before they opened their new Hand of Hope School. Her gaze flicked to the clock on the wall that indicated her elderly driver Hadley was on time to take her home. And not a moment too soon, if this **barbarian** was any indication of the rest of her day.

Her silence apparently **ruffled his fur** because his eyes narrowed, if possible, even more than before as he blasted out a noisy exhale, shaking his head as if *she* were the one with **a pea for a brain**. "Great—a rich dame as dumb as she is lost," he muttered, and every word his insolence had stolen from her lips marched to the tip of her tongue to do battle.

"Pardon me, Mr. Personality," she said in a clipped tone that suggested he'd just **crawled out from under a rock**, "but the one who is lost here, you **cave dweller**, is you, so I suggest you **lumber** back to whatever **cavern** you climbed out of and search for the manners you obviously left behind."

In a royal swoop befitting the new drama teacher of the Hand of Hope School, she snatched the dropped pin from the floor and jabbed it into the bulletin board as if it were the backside of this **unsavory baboon** and every other who'd broken her heart. Before the baboon could speak—**or grunt**—she whirled around with a flourish, satisfied to see **a sagging jaw that likely resembled the mouth of his cave**. She'd obviously rendered the **beast** dumb. *Good—a perfect match for his brain.*

"And for your information, sir, I am the new English and Drama teacher for the Hand of Hope School, so I hardly need some surly wiseacre telling me I'm lost. Because trust me, mister …" Lips pursed, she did a painfully slow perusal from the tip of his pointed head miles down to laced oxford shoes that were surprisingly well polished. Her gaze sailed back up past a lean body with muscled arms and massive shoulders to settle on an annoyingly handsome face. "If I needed a compass, I'd buy one."

The **grouch** caught her totally off-guard when the **sullen slant** of his mouth twitched with a hint of a smile, joining forces with a shuttered look that fluttered her stomach. "I don't care if you teach angels to fly in the wild blue yonder, lady," he said with a flip of a badge. "This is my beat, and you can't park your fancy car out front. It's an annoyance."

Yes, I know the feeling.

⤮⥿

Ahem … yes, so do I, especially when Miss Pepper Basham shoots spitballs in my classroom. She will promptly receive demerits, I assure you. But … writers who enhance the romantic tension in their books via immediate confrontation? Ah … *they* will receive accolades from their readers!

Chapter 12

Making the Most of Touch and Response

Okay, it's time to put your thinking caps on, people, because this chapter is *not* for the faint of heart. Keep in mind that this is inspirational/sweet romance we're talking about here, so we're limited in what we can say and do, and rightfully so.

Consequently, we have to make the most of what we *can* use—the caress of a thumb, a mouth going dry, warm words in an ear, or even a smoldering look. You know what I'm talking about here—the kind of heated look that Collin McGuire gives Faith O'Connor on the cover of *A Passion Most Pure*?

Yeah, well, this chapter is about how we can convey that kind of **look, action, statement,** or **thought** with words that will **"touch"** both the heroine *and* the reader. *Hopefully* to evoke a **"response"** that will create romantic tension and add a little steam to the pages, sometimes *without* even a kiss. This clip from *A Hope Undaunted* is a good example, where the romantic tension between the hero, Luke McGee, and the heroine, Katie O'Connor, "steams" Katie's face because of his veiled reference to a kiss he forced on her earlier in the book. His **"look"** coupled with a very short statement is the thing that **"touches"** the heroine, eliciting an embarrassed **"response"** that heightens the romantic tension.

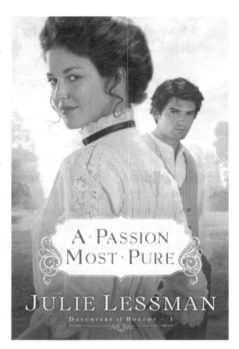

Here are four things I recommend to accomplish this:
1. Utilize beats to heighten the tension.
2. Keep dialogue to a minimum and pivotal responses short.
3. Utilize the power of pauses.
4. Keep a mirror handy to capture exact expressions.

Pay close attention to the hero's lazy smile and telling look in the second example (with beats), accomplished with a pause, a "weighted gaze," and short dialogue.

And, to emphasize the importance of "beats" from chapter two, I'm showing the clip two ways—first without hero beats and then with hero beats. In the first example without hero beats, the veiled tease is not too evident, diminishing the romantic tension, but it is in the second example with hero beats **(bolded)**, so I hope you think so too.

EXAMPLE WITH NO HERO BEATS
Katie frowned at the thick stack of bacon on Luke's burger compared to the two measly pieces on each of hers. "You must have a pound of bacon on that sandwich. For pity's sake, what'd you do, bribe her?"

Julie Lessman

"Bribe her? No, Katydid," Luke said, "because unlike you, some women actually enjoy doing what I ask."

"Ask maybe, but force? Do they enjoy that?"

"Sometimes," he said.

EXAMPLE WITH HERO BEATS (bolded)

Katie's gaze flitted from the thick stack of bacon on Luke's burger to the two measly pieces on each of hers. She frowned. "You must have a pound of bacon on that sandwich. For pity's sake, what'd you do, bribe her?"

Luke lifted the mammoth burger to his lips, pausing to give Katie a weighted gaze. "Bribe her? No, Katydid, because unlike you, some women actually enjoy doing what I ask."

"Ask maybe, but force? Do they enjoy that?"

He bit into his sandwich and chewed slowly, a smile surfacing at the edges of his lips. "Sometimes," he said, heating her with a shuttered look while he took a slow swig of his drink.**

Katie's cheeks flamed hot, and she itched to slap that smug smile off his handsome face. Instead, she whirled around to face Betty. "So, how are the ribs?"

Another way to make the most of "touch and response" is through **"circumstances of close proximity"** that shock or surprise the hero and heroine, such as in the two scenes that follow. The first is from *A Heart Revealed* where the heroine teases the hero by snatching his favorite candy bar from his pocket, allowing a chase to ensue between two people who are "strictly friends." Notice how the heroine's shocked response in the last few paragraphs **(bolded)** in turn elicits a romantically tense response from the hero **(also bolded)** ... *and*, I hope, from the reader.

The thrill of the hunt broadened his grin as he took his time, his gait slow and easy while he rounded her desk, gaze hungry and locked with hers. "Give it back, Mrs. Malloy," he whispered, feeling the adrenaline of horseplay that pumped in his veins.

"No!" she cried, more giggles bubbling over. She jerked her chair to block his way, then eased around the desk, waving the Snickers like a taunt, her impish smile reminding him of Gabe. "Not until you learn the lindy *and* promise to leave the candy at home when you go to this wedding. You may be a late bloomer, but at least you won't smell like a little boy."

That did it. Slamming the chair in, he lunged, surprising her with a firm clasp of her arm. He dove for the Snickers, but she fought him with shrieks of wild laughter, the candy bar clutched tightly behind her back. He reeled her in and grinned, challenge coursing his veins as he gripped her to his chest.

"Give it up, Emma," he breathed, "you won't win." Locking her with one arm, his other circled her waist while his hand wrestled with hers to recapture the candy.

Suddenly her body stilled ... and in a **catch of his breath**, everything changed. One moment she was laughing, and in the next, her **laughter faded away**, leaving her **lips parted with shallow breaths** while gentle **eyes slowly spanned wide**. The effect totally disarmed him, **causing his heart to thud to a stop. Silence pounded in his ears** as he became aware of **her body pressed to his**, her warmth, her scent **engaging his pulse to a degree that jolted him. He swallowed hard, feeling the rise and fall of her chest**, the **burn of her hand embedded in his**, and **a flash of heat** traveled his body until it **scorched in his cheeks. He flinched away.**

"Emma, I'm sorry—I didn't mean to manhandle you." He **stepped back and plunged his hands in his pockets**, desperate to deflect the embarrassment he felt. His smile was awkward. "Keep the candy then, I have more in my bottom drawer."

❧❧

The second example is from *Dare to Love Again* with a **"circumstance of close proximity."** Here we have the heroine accidentally falling from where she is standing on a chair in her classroom, straight into the hero's arms for an "almost kiss." Again, note the **looks, actions, statements,** or **thoughts (all bolded),** which are all credible **"touches"** to draw out a romantically tense **"response."**

He extended his hand with a cock of his head. "May I help you down so we can start over?"

She drew in a deep breath and released it with a nervous smile of relief, placing her palm in his. "Yes, please." Voice as soft as her touch, she startled when the dainty tip of her oxblood kid leather shoe accidentally kicked the pin box to the floor. "Oh!" she squeaked, the crash of the pins apparently leaving her off kilter. With **a look of abject horror**, **she flailed in the air** for several **panicked heartbeats** before finally **thudding hard against his chest**, **his arms fusing them together in a state of mutual stun.**

He blinked, paralyzed by the warmth of her body, the flare of her eyes, the scent of chocolate from parted lips so lush, the fire blazing through him could have melted the candy in her bowl. As if hypnotized by the shape of her mouth, his gaze lingered there, feeling the pull ...

"Uh, Mr. Barone?" **The lips appeared to move in slow motion**, their soft, pink color luring him close ... *so* very close.

"Mmm?" Barely aware, **he felt his body lean in, breathing shallow and eyelids heavy,** that perfect mouth calling him home ...

"Mr. Barone!"

Her tone could have been a whack of her stick, jerking him from his fog with the reminder that a woman still dangled in his arms. **Sucking in a harsh breath, he dropped her to her feet** so fast, the poor thing teetered like his sanity in even thinking about kissing a dame from Snob Hill.

❧❧

In summation, there are a wide array of tricks in your bag to heighten romantic tension other than the "kiss," from romantically tense **circumstances of proximity** to **looks, actions, statements,** or **thoughts,** so explore the possibilities and have fun!

Chapter 13

Implementing the Concept of Forbidden Fruit

Mercy me—forbidden fruit! Oh my, it got Adam and Eve in trouble in the Garden of Eden and trust me, people, it will get your characters in trouble too—with romantic tension almost too hot to handle!!

In *A Heart Revealed*, I had to tread lightly because my heroine was married, so even the hint of impropriety between her and the unmarried hero stirs the tension between these two close friends. Which is why the following love scene did not happen right away in the book, but when it did, the temptation of forbidden fruit, no matter how innocent, serves to ratchet the romantic tension above and beyond a normal love scene. In this clip, we have the hero, Sean O'Connor, comforting the heroine, Emma Malloy, after she's badly hurt in an accident. Please note that in the full context of the book, both the hero and heroine actually honor the bonds of marriage for the sake of God and each other.

Her body shuddered against his chest as she clung to him, the scent of soap and Snickers as soothing as the warm palm that kneaded the nape of her neck.

"Shh . . . shh . . . it's okay, Emma . . ." He fanned his fingers through her hair, then cupped her face in his palms, his gaze a tender caress. "I'm here now," he whispered, kissing her forehead, her temple, her cheek . . .

Her pulse quickened while her weeping stilled to soft, little heaves, and as her eyelids drifted closed, her heart stuttered when he brushed them with his lips.

"I'll keep you safe, I promise," he whispered, and a silent moan faded in her throat as his mouth trailed to her temple. "I swear no one will ever hurt you again . . ."

Heat throbbed within as she lost herself in the caress of his hand, her mind dazed while his mouth explored. The soft flesh of her ear, the curve of her throat, her body humming with need as never before. She felt his shallow breaths, warm against her skin, and with a low groan, he cradled her neck to capture her mouth with his own. "Oh, Emma," he whispered, his voice hoarse against her lips, "I want to be there always, to protect you, cherish you . . ." He deepened his kiss, and she tasted the salt of her tears.

All reason fled and she was lost, the air hitching in her throat a mere heartbeat before she returned his passion, her mouth warm beneath his. She knew it had never been like this with anyone—not with Rory or others or even in her wildest dreams. A merging of souls as well as bodies, where hope soared and love swelled in her chest until she thought she would burst.

Sean—*her Sean*—tasting her like this, loving her like this, felt so right, so natural, the missing piece of her soul. Kisses both tender and hungry, uniting them, changing them, molding friends into lovers for the rest of their lives …

"God, forgive me," she whispered, her body shivering from the caress of his mouth to her throat. Her words vibrated beneath his lips, fragile and tinged with awe. "I never knew … never dreamed … it could be like this …"

He clutched her close, his uneven breathing in rhythm with hers. "Emma, I'm so stupid—I never saw this coming, but God help me … I'm in love with you."

No! She jolted away, his words searing her conscience with a pain more awful than the accident had inflicted. Fear clawed in her throat, forcing her back against the wooden arms of the couch. "No, Sean, please—you can't!"

He stared, his face filled with grief. "It's too late," he whispered. "I can't not love you—not now, not after this."

"But it's wrong!" She put a hand to her neck, her chest heaving and her mind convulsing with guilt. *God, how could I have done this?* Tears stung her eyes as self-loathing rose in her throat like bile. She was everything Rory had branded her—a liar and a whore, scarred and hideous, not fit for any man's bed. She looked away, nauseous at the thought that Sean might see her for the vile woman she was. Her voice shuddered with shame. "We can't do this, Sean, ever—do you hear? I gave my vow to Rory, and you need to marry Rose. You belong with her."

Tragedy welled in his eyes as he shook his head. "No, Emma, I belong with you …"

෧෯

Forbidden fruit—like forbidden gum in the classroom—although sticky to do, definitely gives the reader something extra to chew on in the realm of romantic tension.

Chapter 14

Words with a Hint of Taboo

Miss Basham—close the door and lock it please, and Miss Crandall, crank the record player up to muffle what I'm about to say. Because you people need to know there are words out there that heat up romantic tension a little more than others just by their shock value alone. You know what I mean—questionable words like *lust, lover, sensual, fondle, make love*"—each conveying a passion that borders on taboo in inspirational romance. Words like this are sometimes needed to emphasize an undesirable mindset of a rogue hero who eventually changes throughout the course of the book or even to inject a sense of danger into a scene. Consequently, just the hint of shock in these words can infuse romantic tension into a scene without ever venturing beyond, as I will demonstrate in the clips below.

In this scene from *A Passion Most Pure*, the hero, Collin McGuire, and the heroine, Faith O'Connor, are in a heated argument because he loves her and she loves him, but she refuses to marry him because of his lack of faith in God. I'm going to do the scene two ways—example A with the word *lover* and example B without. You be the judge as to which sample more closely depicts the rogue intent of our bad-boy hero *and* elicits the most romantic tension and shock factor.

EXAMPLE A (with the word *lover*)

He heard her move toward him. "You know, Collin, someday we'll be friends—good friends."

His eyes flew open, and he didn't blink once. "I don't want to be your friend, Faith. I want to be your husband and your **lover.**"

A dark blush invaded her cheeks. She lifted her chin. "Me, too, Collin, more than anything in the world."

He heaved the chair against the table again, the sound as explosive as the fire in his gut. "That's a lie!"

EXAMPLE A (without the word *lover*)

He heard her move toward him. "You know, Collin, someday we'll be friends—good friends."

His eyes flew open, and he didn't blink once. "I don't want to be your friend, Faith. I want to be your husband."

She lifted her chin. "Me, too, Collin, more than anything in the world."

He heaved the chair against the table again, the sound as explosive as the fire in his gut. "That's a lie!"

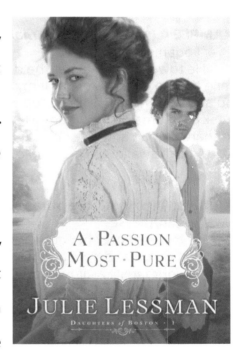

Julie Lessman

In this next scene from *A Passion Most Pure*, the hero is reflecting on his love for the heroine. Again, I will present the clip two ways—example A with the words *lust* and *bad girl*, and example B without. You tell me which has more punch.

EXAMPLE A (with the words *lust* and *bad girl*)

He was in love and knew it. Certainly he'd been in lust enough times to know the difference. She was truly remarkable--a woman who had all the passion of a bad girl and all the restraint of an angel. For him, it was a deadly combination, and one that convinced him his days of bachelorhood were numbered.

EXAMPLE B (without the words *lust* and *bad girl*)

He was in love and knew it. Certainly he'd seen enough women to know the difference. She was truly remarkable--a passionate woman with all the restraint of an angel. For him, it was a deadly combination, and one that convinced him his days of bachelorhood were numbered.

❧❧

In these two scenes from *Dare to Love Again*, the subordinate hero Logan McClare is angry with the subordinate heroine Caitlyn McClare because she rejected his proposal of marriage. Note the intensity of example A, which includes the phrase *make love* versus example B that does not.

EXAMPLE A (with the phrase *make love*)

"Logan, please—"

He towered over her at the door, anger fairly shimmering off his body. "Please what, Cait? Smile and go on as before as if my heart hasn't been ripped out? Laugh and talk and dine with you and your family as if my hopes haven't just been crushed? Give you a lifeless peck on the cheek each time I leave when all I really want to do is make love to you night after night in a bed we share as man and wife?"

A flush swallowed her whole.

EXAMPLE A (without the phrase *make love*)

"Logan, please—"

He towered over her at the door, anger fairly shimmering off his body. "Please what, Cait? Smile and go on as before as if my heart hasn't been ripped out? Laugh and talk and dine with you and your family as if my hopes haven't just been crushed? Give you a lifeless peck on the cheek each time I leave, knowing we will never be man and wife?"

A flush swallowed her whole.

❧❧

Finally, note the subtle difference in this clip from *A Heart Revealed* when the hero is trying to make up with his wife and "suckles" her ear versus just "kissing" it.

EXAMPLE A (with the word *suckle*)

"Oh, no you don't, McGee," she hissed, thrashing her head side to side. "You are not going to sweet-talk me now—"

He silenced her with a kiss that nearly consumed him, and his breathing was heavy as his mouth slid to suckle the lobe of her ear. "Come on, Katie," he whispered, "let's kiss and make up …"

EXAMPLE B (without the word *suckle*)

"Oh, no you don't, McGee," she hissed, thrashing her head side to side. "You are not going to sweet-talk me now—"

He silenced her with his lips, his breathing heavy as his mouth slid to kiss the lobe of her ear. "Come on, Katie," he whispered, "let's kiss and make up …"

So remember, like the perfume with a similar name, sometimes just a hint of "taboo" is enough to permeate the scene with the subtle scent of romantic tension.

Chapter 15

Appropriate "Bleep" Words for Inspirational Romance

BAM! Okay, spit out the gum, cut the chatter, and eyes up front. What you see here on my desk, people, is a bar of soap, which I don't expect to need today because there will be no profanity in my classroom—*or* the inspirational or sweet markets for that matter, understood? Nobody reading inspirational or sweet romance today wants to fill their minds with a bunch of offensive words, but what's an author to do when the situation calls for it?

Good question. Keep in mind, I am not advocating profanity in novels, especially inspirational novels, but I do believe that sometimes "strong" language is a must in effective storytelling. Let's face it, can you imagine Rhett Butler saying "Frankly, my dear, I don't give a rat's tail" to Scarlett as he walks out the door? Of course not! So, just how do you interject believable tension in a scene that calls for a character to swear or scream at someone? Well, trust me—it's not easy, but it is doable.

Here's an example from *A Passion Most Pure* where the hero is intensely frustrated. In the first example, the phrase "blast it all" helps to underscore that frustration and emphasize it, whereas the second example without it falls a little flat.

EXAMPLE A (with the phrase *blast it all*)

Mitch dragged his fingers through his hair. **Blast it all,** it was one thing to stop seeing other women now that he had Faith, but it was something else altogether when the temptation was right under your nose, so close—and so willing—you could almost touch it.

EXAMPLE B (without the phrase *blast it all*)

Mitch dragged his fingers through his hair. It was one thing to stop seeing other women now that he had Faith, but it was something else altogether when the temptation was right under your nose, so close—and so willing—you could almost touch it.

❧✺

In this second clip from *Love at Any Cost,* the hero expresses his anger and disbelief in the first example with the phrase "the deuce it is," whereas in the second example, there's no passion behind his anger without that phrase.

EXAMPLE A (with the phrase *the deuce it is*)

"Their caseload is full and there's nothing they can do." He snatched the letter and sailed it into the waste can. "The deuce it is," he growled, resting his head on the back of his chair. He closed his eyes. "It's full all right—with Nob Hill favors."

Julie Lessman

EXAMPLE B (without the phrase *the deuce it is*)
"Their caseload is full and there's nothing they can do." He snatched the letter and sailed it into the waste can. He rested his head on the back of his chair and closed his eyes. "It's full all right—with Nob Hill favors."

৵৽

In this final clip from *A Passion Most Pure,* the heroine is a godly young woman with a deep faith who would never utter a foul word to anybody. But she has been so badly wounded by the hero that both her heart and her faith are crushed. Her response in telling the hero to "go to the devil" is not only necessary for shock value to demonstrate just how much this wound has hurt her, but also how much it has changed her and her faith.

EXAMPLE A (with the phrase *go to the devil*)
"When will you leave?"
Faith's eyes flitted to her mother's tired form bent over the bed. She felt a sudden prick of tears in her eyes. Her lips pressed tight. She could not allow her love for her mother to deter her from her rage. She must guard it at all costs—it made her strong. It ensured she would go. "This weekend," she lied.
Her mother nodded, slowly rising to her feet. "What will I tell Mitch?" she whispered.
Faith eyed her mother with cool indifference. "Tell him to go to the devil," she said, and meant it. And the look on her mother's face was worth the price.

EXAMPLE B (without the phrase *go to the devil*)
Her mother nodded, slowly rising to her feet. "What will I tell Mitch?" she whispered.
Faith eyed her mother with cool indifference. "Tell him I don't want to see him again," she said, and meant it. And the look on her mother's face was worth the price.

৵৽

Oh, phooey—we're out of time for today, but as an extra bonus, I am including my own personal lists of bleep words, most of which will provide tension when needed without being offensive to most publishers in the inspirational or sweet markets.

Mild Derogatory Names

Animal
Blackguard
Bloodsucking, lowlife abuser
Boor
Bozo
Brickhead
Cad
Charlatan
Creep
Dingleberry
Dipstick
Dip Wad
Dirtbag
Festering, rotting piece of filth
Flea-infested varmint
Fraud
Goon
Hack
Idiot
Ignoramus
Insufferable wretch
Knothead
Knucklehead
Load of human pus
Low-down, mealy-mouth coyote
Low-down skunk
Lower than a snake's belly in a wagon rut
Lower than slime a snail leaves behind
Lowlife
Mangy, flea-infested dog
Mangy mutt
Menace
Mongrel
Mule-brained
Mutt
No-count swindler
Nose-picker
Numb-skull
Odious toad
Pain in the backside
Pain in the neck
Pain in the rump
Pest
Phony
Pickle brain
Pickle head
Pig-headed

Polecat
Ragamuffin
Reprobate
Rogue
Sap
Scallywag
Scamp
Scumbag
Scum ball
Scum-bucket
Scuz bucket
Shyster
Slime
Slime ball
Slime bucket
Snake
Snake belly
Son of an unnamed goat
Troublemaker
Two-bit grease ball
Two-bit turkey
Varlet
Varmint
Waste of good air
Waste of oxygen
Weasel
Wet blanket
Wise guy
Womanizer
Worm
Worthless sack of dung
Yellow-bellied, wart-covered toad

Mild Expressions

Bah, humbug
Balderdash
Baloney
Bee's knees
Blamed
Blame it
Blast
Blasted
Blazes
Blessed
Bless her heart
Blimey
Blinkin'
Bloomin'
Bloomin' saints
Blue blazes
Blue-blistering barnacles
Blue-blistering blazes
Botheration
Boy howdy
Buggeration
By jingo
By thunder
Claptrap
Confound it
Consternation
Criminently
Criminy
Crumb
Curses
Dadburnit
Dadgum
Dash
Dash it
Dash it all
Deuce
Dirty word, dirty word, dirty word
Doggone it
Double sugar
Drat
Drawers of the devil
Egad
Fiddle-dee-dee
Fiddle-faddle
Fiddlesticks
Flat tire
For crying out loud

For crying out loud in a bucket
For heaven's sake
For mercy's sake
For pity's sake
For the love of all that is good and decent
For the love of Ivy
For the love of Job
For the sake of the heavenly host
Gad
Gadzooks
Gee whiz
Gee willickers
Geez Louise
Glory be
Go to thunder
Go to the devil
Golly
Golly gee
Good gracious
Good gravy
Good grief
Good heavenly days
Goodness knows
Good night
Gosh
Great balls of fire
Great Caesar's ghost
Great day in the morning
Great Jehoshaphat
Great Scott
Hang it all
Heaven forbid
Heaven knows
Heavens to Betsy!
Hell's teeth
Holy blazes
Holy cats
Holy cow
Holy mackerel
Holy smoke
Holy thunder
Holy-moly
Horsefeathers
Humbug
Hum-dinghies
I'll be jiggered
Infernal

Jeepers creepers
Jiminy
Jubilation
Jumping Jehoshaphat
Jumpin' toadstools
Land sake
Lawdy
Lordy be
Man alive
Merciful heavens
Merciful providence
Mercy
Mercy me
Mercy sake
My stars and garters
My word
Nonsense
Nuts
Oh, crumb
Oh, fiddle
Oh, for crying out loud
Oh, fudge
Oh, go shoot yourself in the foot
Oh, my cow
Oh, my stars
Oh, my stars and garters
Oh, my word
Oh, piddle
Oh, rats
Oh, sugar
Perdition
Phoo
Phooey
Pish-posh
Pooh
Poop
Poppycock
Rats
Rats, rats, rats
Saints alive
Saints almighty
Sakes alive
Shirts and skirts
Shucks
Son-of-a biscuit-eater
St. Peter's gate
St. Peter's nightgown
Sweet heavenly days
Sweet mother of Job
Sweet mother of mercy

Sweet mother of pearl
Sweet onions
Sweet saints
Sweet suffering saints
Sweet Texas tea
Tarnation
Thank goodness
The deuce it is
The dickens
Thunderation
Upon my word
Well I'll be
Well I'll be horn-swaggled
Well knock me down and steal my teeth
Well, shut my mouth
What in the Sam Hill
What the blazes
Whoopie
Wow
Ye gods

Chapter 16

KISS-ology 101: The Many Faces of a Kiss

FIELD TRIP!! Now that we've covered most of the basics, it's time for a little fun with examples of various types of love scenes from my novels that have earned me the nickname of the "Kissing Queen" of inspirational romance. I've even heard the rumor that some of you actually use my novels as a handbook for writing love scenes, so let's just make it easy for everyone, shall we? Here's a sampling of my various styles of kisses. Miss Perry—turn on the fan, if you please.

THE ACCIDENTAL KISS

Come on, you know what I'm talking about—the "accidental kiss" is when the attraction is there, but the intent isn't . . . *until* something as innocent as a kiss on the cheek sets passion ablaze. In a second-tier love story from *Love at Any Cost*, an innocent thank-you kiss on the cheek turns into far more between the widowed matriarch and her rogue brother-in-law—the fiancé she was once engaged to before he cheated on her and she married his brother. Bundled in a blanket around an outside fire, Caitlyn McClare rises to thank her brother-in-law Logan with a kiss on the cheek for a tender and noble gift he'd just given her.

> Peering up, Caitlyn gently braced his jaw with her palm, eyes shimmering with gratitude. "I don't think I've ever loved you more than right this moment, Logan McClare. Thank you!"
>
> His heart seized when she pressed a kiss to his cheek, and almost by accident, he turned into her silky caress, their lips so close he could smell the hint of hot chocolate they'd enjoyed around the fire. They froze in the same split second of time, and his pulse thudded slow and hard as he waited for her to pull away. Only she didn't, and heat scorched his body when her shallow breathing warmed his skin.
>
> "Cait," he whispered, barely believing her lips nearly grazed his. All he could hear was the roar of blood in his ears as he waited, not willing to push for fear she would bolt, but when her eyelids flickered closed, his fate was sealed. "So help me, Cait, I love you," he rasped, nuzzling her lips before she could retreat. The moment his mouth took hers, he was a man hopelessly lost, bewitched by her spell.
>
> She jolted in his arms as if suddenly realizing her folly, but he refused to relent, his grip at the nape of her neck strong and sure. A delicious dizziness overtook him at the taste of the sweetest lips he'd ever known, a heady tease of chocolate and peppermint and Caitlyn McClare. A groan trapped in his throat, and he devoured her, delving deeper with a passion stoked by almost twenty-six years of denial and longing. "God help me, Cait," he whispered, voice hoarse as he feathered her ear, "I need you in my life."
>
> He felt it the moment the winds shifted, pulse skyrocketing when her blanket dropped to the ground and she melded into his arms. His mouth explored with a vengeance, the frenzied beat of her heart throbbing beneath his lips as he grazed the hollow of her throat. He skimmed up to suckle the lobe of her ear, and his heart swelled with joy when a soft moan escaped her lips. Blood pounding in his veins, he wove fingers into her hair to cradle her face. "Marry me, Cait, please . . ."

Julie Lessman

Her eyelids fluttered open to reveal a glaze of desire so strong, his mouth descended again, dominant and possessive until her lips surrendered to his. "Marry me," he repeated, his kiss gentling to playful nips meant to coax and tease. "I need you, Cait . . . and I *want* you."

In the space of a heartbeat, she hurled him away, breasts heaving and eyes wild. "You're a devil, Logan McClare, always lusting after what you can't have!"

Sleet slithered through his veins. "No, Cait, it's not true—I want you because I love you."

He reached for her, and she thrust back, fury welling in her eyes. "You want me because you can't have me. And once you had me, you would just throw me away again, returning to your old habits of carousing with women all hours of the night."

"You're wrong—let me prove it, please. Marry me."

She shook her head, a scarlet curl quivering against her neck. Her tone trembled with a violence that stunned. "I-don't-want-you, and I-don't-need-you, do you hear?"

His anger surged, but he tamped it down with a clamp of his jaw, his words as hard as hers. "Really, Cait? Why don't you tell that to the woman whose body just responded to mine?"

The lightening force of her slap shifted his jaw clean to the right, the sound of it like a crack of thunder. "How dare you?" she whispered, tears streaming her cheeks.

THE CAVEMAN KISS

Okay, I'm pretty sure I always get an eye-roll from my editor every time I write what I call the "caveman kiss," which is when a hero takes a kiss by force, dominating the heroine to stake his claim. You know, like in those wonderful old-fashioned movies when John Wayne would lay one on Maureen O'Hara in *McClintock,* or when Rhett drags Scarlett from the wagon to steal a kiss on a sunset hill in *Gone with the Wind*? Or even like that classic pic of the soldier kissing a nurse in the street—a perfect stranger—following the armistice for WWII?

Sigh. Call me old-fashioned, but I love the stolen kiss, although I do realize it's not always politically or socially correct in today's world where things like spousal abuse and date rape are a sad reality. Please note—in no way do I condone either of these types of behavior nor are my scenes meant to be perceived as such. They are written in the old-fashioned "Calgon, take me away" style of romance so prevalent in the old Hollywood movies and in absolutely every case, the dominant hero is called to task for his behavior and eventually learns from it.

In this billiard-room scene from *Love at Any Cost*, the hero is a pretty-boy rogue bent on turning the head of our heroine who wants nothing to do with him. After she stomps on his pride and trips his temper, he opts for vindication with a stolen kiss, for which he pays dearly with a kick in the ankle, a knee in the thigh, and the heroine's disdain for the next month.

He grinned, eyes never straying as he chalked his cue. "Up for a game?"

"With you?" She arched a brow. "No, thank you, I don't play games with men like you."

Ouch. She was obviously a woman who was honest and forthright, what you see is what you get, and so help him, what he saw, he definitely wanted. But . . . she didn't want him. *Yet.* He softened his approach. "Come on, Cassie, one game of eight ball isn't going to kill you, and then you'll have the chance to give me the thrashing I so richly deserve."

She hung her head and huffed out a sigh, finally meeting his gaze with a candid one of her own. "Mr. MacKenna—"

"Jamie—please."

"Jamie, then . . . ," she began slowly, as if attempting to ease the blow of what she was about to say. Sympathy radiated from those remarkable green eyes that reminded him so much of a pure mountain stream—unspoiled, refreshing. *And* icy enough to tingle the skin. Long lashes flickered as if begging him to understand. "Look, no offense, but you just broke my heart."

He blinked. "Pardon me?"

"Oh, not you exactly," she said, dismissing him with a wave of her hand, "but a man just like you—you know, handsome, smart, the kind that melts a woman with a smile?"

A ridge popped at the bridge of his nose. "Uh, thank you—I guess?"

She looked up then, head tilted in much the same way a mother might soothe a child, expression kind and tone, parental. "Look, I'm sure you're a very nice person, Jamie MacKenna, and we may even forge a friendship before summer is through, but you need to understand something right now if that friendship is ever going to see the light of day."

She took his hand in hers, patting it as if he were five years old, and in all of his twenty-five years, never had a woman given him a more patronizing smile. "You have zero chance ..." She held up a hand, index finger and thumb circled to create an O, then enunciated slowly as if he were one of the livestock back on her ranch. "Zee-ro chance of *ever* turning my head because I have no interest in you or any man right now, especially a pretty boy." She gave him a patient smile edged with just enough pity to get on his nerves. "I'm sorry to be so blunt, but I see no point in hemming and hawing around a pesky hornet when I can just stomp on it before it stings."

His jaw sagged. "Hornet?" He'd been called a lot of things, but somehow, out of the pursed lips of this Texas beauty, this stung his pride more than the blasted hornet. A nerve pulsed in his cheek as he replaced his cue in the rack, his smile cool. "Is that so? And what makes you think I have any interest in turning your head?"

She folded her arms again and hiked one beautiful brow, daring him to deny it.

And, oh, how he wanted to. His jaw began to grind. But he couldn't because it would be a bald-faced lie, and they both knew it. He exhaled and pinched the bridge of his nose, finally huffing out a sigh. "Okay, you're right, Miss McClare—I was trying to turn your head. But I'm not stupid—I can see you obviously have no interest in me whatsoever."

"None," she confirmed, brows arched high in agreement.

He nodded, head bowed as he kneaded the back of his neck. "Which means, of course, there's no attraction whatsoever ..."

"Oh, heaven forbid." Her body shivered in revulsion. "Not in a million years ..."

He stared, a trace of hurt in his tone. "Nothing—not even a glimmer?"

She shook her head, face scrunched as if she tasted something bad. "Good gracious, no."

He exhaled loudly. "All righty, then," he said with a stiff smile, his pride effectively trampled. Rubbing his temple, he supposed there was only one thing left to do. He extended his palm with a conciliatory smile. "Well, I'm glad we got that out of the way. So ... friends?"

She stared at his hand as if it were a rattler about to strike, then shifted her gaze to his, lids narrowing the slightest bit. Absently scraping her lip, she tentatively placed her hand in his.

His fingers closed around hers and he smiled. *Ah, sweet vindication ...*

In a sharp catch of her breath, he jerked her to him so hard, the cue in her hand literally spiraled across the plush burgundy carpet. Thudding against his chest, she emitted a soft, little grunt, and her outraged protest was lost in his mouth, the sweet taste of her lips shocking him even more than he had shocked her. She tried to squirm away and he cupped her neck with a firm hold and gentle dominance, deepening the kiss.

A grunt broke from his mouth when her foot near broke his ankle. "I'll tell you what, Miss McClare," he said, teeth clenched as pain seared his leg, "I'll give you feisty ..."

"You ... haven't ... *seen* ... feisty," she rasped, flailing in his arms. With another sharp jolt of pain, she cocked a very unladylike knee into his left thigh, stealing his wind while her words hissed in his face. "Oh ... why ... didn't ... I wear ... my boots ..."

Because it's my lucky day? Jamie grimaced, determined to prove the lady a liar, at least on the score of attraction. Body and mind steeled to win, he jerked her flush and kissed her hard while she pummeled his shoulders in a flurry of fists. All at once, her scent disarmed him—a hint

Julie Lessman

of lilacs and soap and the barest trace of peppermint, and he stifled a groan while he explored the shape of her mouth, the silk of her skin, the soft flesh of her ear.

Relief flooded when her thrashing slowed and her body listed against his with a weak moan. He gentled his mouth, softly nuzzling before finally pulling away. Satisfaction inched into a smile when she swayed on her feet, eyes closed and open mouth as limp as her body. "Nope, not in a million years," he said, his breathing as shallow as hers. He planted a kiss to her nose.

Roused from her stupor, her eyes popped open in shock and she suddenly lunged, fury sputtering as she hauled back a fist, clearly hoping to dislocate his jaw. With all the grace and speed of his Oly Club boxing title, he skillfully ducked, chuckling when her tight-knuckled punch bludgeoned the air. Hands in his pockets, he made his way to the door and delivered a gloat of grin over his shoulder. "Well, I guess you have a deal, then, Cassie McClare—friends it is."

She spun around, eyes flashing. "You are nothing but a yellow-bellied snake of a womanizer, Jamie MacKenna, and if you ever lay a finger on me again, I'll hogtie you so fast ..."

He laughed, hand on the knob. "Come on, Your Highness, I did us both a favor—now that we know there's no attraction, we can be friends, right?"

"When polecats fly," she screamed, and he grinned, shutting the door with a wink. Something hard crashed against the wood and he winced. "Yes, ma'am," he whispered to himself on his way down the hall. "Definitely the makings of a beautiful friendship."

THE COAXING KISS

In this scene from *A Hope Undaunted*, the hero, Luke McGee, is hoping to coax the heroine, Katie O'Connor, into dating him, unaware she has just accepted an engagement ring from her boyfriend Jack.

Glass in hand, she paused at the sink. "Do you want ice?"

His approach was achingly slow as he strolled toward her. With a casual air, he took the glass from her hand and set it on the counter while his warm gaze welded to hers. He moved in close, wedging her against the sink by just the mere threat of his presence. She swallowed hard and craned her neck up, wishing her voice hadn't fused to her throat.

Massive palms slowly grazed the side of her arms, as if he thought she might be chilled, but the heat they generated made her feel anything but. In fluid motion, they moved to her waist, the gentle caress of his thumbs all but stealing her air. His blue eyes deepened in intensity as he leaned in, and his husky voice made her mouth go dry. "Let's face it, Katie Rose," he whispered, "I don't want ice, I don't want water, and I definitely don't want chocolate."

She caught her breath when his words melted warm in her ear.

"I want you ..."

And before the air could return to her lungs, his mouth dominated hers with such gentle force, it coaxed a breathless moan from her lips, heating the blood in her veins by several degrees. "Say it, Katie Rose ... say that you want me as much as I want you."

She could barely speak for the racing of her pulse, and her breathing was as rapid as his. Powerful arms refused to relent, drawing her close as his lips trailed her throat with an urgency that made her dizzy. "Say it," he whispered again, "tell me you care for me too."

"Luke, I—I ... I do," she breathed, too disarmed to deny it.

His mouth took hers like a man possessed, deepening the kiss until she was putty in his hands. And then all at once, he pulled away to cup her face with his palms, his eyes so full of love, it took her breath away. "That's all I needed to know, Katie. And I promise from now on, I'll be taking it slow. I don't want to rush this."

She blinked, her pulse thudding to a stop. "Rush what?"

He bent to give her a warm, unhurried kiss. "Us," he whispered against her mouth. "I'm in love with you, Katie Rose."

THE KISS-AND-MAKE-UP KISS

There is almost nothing I would rather write than a kiss-and-make-up scene following a horrendous fight. There's just something about those rollercoaster emotions—from anger, to apology, to love—that makes me want to swoon. A good example is this scene from *A Hope Undaunted*, which happens to be Principal Mooney's favorite love scene in all of my books. Here we have the subordinate hero Patrick O'Connor attempting to comfort his wife Marcy after a volatile argument.

He bludgeoned his pillow and edged away once again. Tears spilled as she stared, the muscles of his body as rigid and hard as his words. With a broken sob, she fell on her pillow, forcing violent heaves to shiver their bed.

Painful seconds elapsed before she felt him move beside her. Her body jerked at the touch of his hand, and like a wounded animal, she curled her knees to her chest.

"Marcy—" The pull of his hand drew her close, and she fought him with flailing arms. His hold became like steel casing, crushing her close, and the chaotic beat of his heart pulsed in her ears. "Marcy," he whispered into the curve of her neck, "I'm sorry. We'll talk this through, I promise. But please, darlin', no more crying—you're breaking my heart."

Moments passed before her sobs finally stilled and all energy drained from her body. With soothing whispers, Patrick kissed her brow, her cheek, her lips—gentle brushes all, laden with repentance. He cupped her jaw in the palm of his hand and fondled her lips with a gentle caress, then pulled away to plead with his eyes. "Marcy, I was wrong. Blame it on poor temper from a bad game of chess or the dip in the stock market, but I overreacted badly, and I'm sorry. But we need to come to terms over Gabe, or I worry we may have more than a fight on our hands."

She sniffed, and he leaned back to retrieve his handkerchief from the nightstand. He handed it to her, and she blew her nose, all anger finally diffused. "I-I know, and I'm s-sorry too. We need to work in tandem, I realize, but sometimes it's so hard because I just want to love her."

He gently pushed the hair from her eyes. "You're a loving woman, darlin', which comes in handy with a lout like me, but with a strong-willed child like Gabe, it needs to be coupled with discipline." He lifted her chin with his finger. "We have to present a united front, my love, and you need to learn to say 'no.' Or I'm afraid with Gabe, there will be a heavy price to pay."

She nodded and sniffed again.

With a tight squeeze, he buried his head in her neck before pulling away with a lift of his brow. He stared at her new satin gown, then slowly fanned his hands down the sides of her waist. "And speaking of a price to pay—so you've taken to wearing perfume to bed, have you, Mrs. O'Connor?" He bent to caress the curve of her throat while his fingers grazed the strap of her gown. "And a new satin gown, surely not just for sleep." With a slow sweep of his thumb, the strap slithered from her shoulder. "Oh, I'm afraid this is going to cost you, darlin'."

He kissed her full on the mouth, and heat shivered through her. "I suppose this isn't one of those times when I need to say no," she whispered, her breathing ragged against his jaw.

"No, darlin', it's not." And clutching her close, he fisted the satin gown and moved in to deepen the kiss, his husky words melting into her mouth. "For all the good it would do."

THE KISS OF DESPERATION

In *A Passion Most Pure*, it's Good Friday and war on Germany has just been declared by the U.S. The subordinate heroine Marcy O'Connor begs her husband to stay and comfort her rather than go into work, but when he tries to put her off, she resorts to a kiss of desperation.

Patrick smiled, a rush of love welling his heart. "Marcy, what if I took an extended lunch hour today? You know, between noon and 3:00 p.m.?"

She lunged, almost tipping the chair with her embrace, kissing him with such passion, a soft moan escaped his lips. "Mmmm … maybe I won't go in at all!" he teased, returning her kiss with equal passion. He paused and drew back, a brow shifting high. "You do realize, of course, I'll have to work a bit later tonight, don't you?"

She nodded and kissed him again, and he chuckled at her little-girl enthusiasm. Patting her on the leg, he resumed an air of responsibility. "I'd best be going, then; I'll need every minute I have at work."

Instead of getting up, Marcy pressed closer, her lips swaying against his.

Patrick groaned and nudged her away. "Marcy, you're a wicked woman," he said with a tight grin. "Darlin', there's no time—" He stopped, his heart flinching at the desperation on her face while her eyes pooled with dread.

"Patrick," she pleaded, "*please* … the world's being torn apart at the seams. I *need* to be close to you … *to hold you.* God help us, we're at war! And we don't know what tomorrow might bring …"

The reality of her words stung, and he felt his perspective shift. He picked her up in his arms and kissed her again before letting her go. Pulling his suit coat off the back of the chair, he slung it over his shoulder and took her hand in his, quietly leading the way to their room.

THE MENTAL KISS

To me, one of the most effective ways to add romantic tension is by starting out with an innocent scene that escalates into fun or frenzy. Then, in a single throb of a pulse, it culminates in the moment when both parties suddenly realize an attraction. An attraction so strong, the mental desire for a kiss creates a spark of romantic tension without one lip ever touching the other.

This is what I was striving for in this scene from *A Light in the Window: An Irish Love Story* (the prequel love story of a much younger Marcy and Patrick from the Daughters of Boston and Winds of Change series). The hero and heroine experience that taut moment where a mental kiss teeters on the threshold of action. It all happens during a water fight between two "friends" doing the dishes at the church soup kitchen where they both volunteer.

Her laughter turned to squeals when she tried to get away, but he clamped a steel arm to her waist while he held the rag dangerously close to her neck. "Repeat after me, Marceline," he whispered, eyes issuing a challenge. "Patrick, I'm a brat, I'm sorry, and I will never do this again."

Pulse sprinting, she giggled, eyes flicking from him to the rag in his hand, weighing her options. "And if I don't?"

One dark brow jutted high as his smile eased into a grin. "You won't have to bathe tonight, darlin'."

His words warmed both her cheeks and her temper. "You wouldn't," she dared.

"Only one way to find out." There was a bit of the devil in his eye, the rag dangling precariously close to her neck.

Marcy sucked in a deep breath. "All right, Patrick," she said, skin tingling with mischief and eye on the rag, "I'm a brat, I'm sorry, and I … *won't* promise …" Lunging, she whipped the rag from his hands so fast, he never saw it coming, christening him with dirty dishwater like Father Fitz christened babies in the back of the church.

He hooked her waist before she could escape, and her high-pitch giggles merged with his husky laughter as she flailed in his arms, a death grip on the soppy rag thrashing over their heads. Dishwater flew every which way while he tried to reclaim it, but Marcy hid it behind her back with squeals of laughter. Locking her to his chest with one arm, he circled her waist with his other, his breath warm on her cheek as he grappled to claim the win.

Near breathless, she tried to wrestle free. "Give ... it ... up ... Patrick," she said, her words punctuated by shrieks and shallow rasps. "You will ... never, ever win ..."

Her words seemed to paralyze him, and in a single heave of her breath, his body stilled against hers. She could feel the ragged rise and fall of his chest, the hot press of his arm at the small of her back, the wild hammering of her pulse in her ears. All at once, she was painfully aware of his nearness, bare inches away from the dark stubble that peppered his jaw. His hard-muscled chest was so close she could almost feel the dampness of his shirt while the familiar scent of spices and pine whirled her senses. His breathing was ragged like hers, warm and sweet with the faint scent of chocolate from his chocolate cream pie, and when his gaze lowered to her lips, heat coiled through her so strong, it sapped all moisture from her throat.

The silence roared like the blood in her ears as he stared, a battle waging in his eyes that eclipsed to a dark fervor, shocking her when it quivered her belly. "I will never give up, Marceline," he whispered, his lips parted to emit shallow breaths. Fire singed when his glance flickered to her mouth.

"T-take it ...," she whispered, alarm curling in her stomach. *Dear Lord, had he meant to kiss me?* Prodding the rag to his chest, she pushed him away while heat throbbed in her cheeks. She took an awkward step back, gaze on the floor as she buffed at her arms with brisk motion. "Goodness, Miss Clara will have our heads," she said with nervous chuckle, unable to look at him even yet. "You win, Patrick—I surrender." She forced a casual tone and attempted to sidestep him on her way to the broom closet.

Her heart seized when he halted her with a gentle hand. "Marcy ..." His voice was somber and steeped with regret. "I'm sorry ..."

"For what?" A deep voice sounded from the door, shattering what was left of Marcy's calm.

THE MISTAKEN-IDENTITY KISS

The element of surprise is always fun in a mistaken-identity kiss, such as in this scene from *A Passion Most Pure* where the hero Collin McGuire mistakes the heroine Faith O'Connor for her sister.

"Stay, Barney," she whispered, silently opening the door to slip outside. The chill of the night air shivered through her, and she pulled her robe tighter about her, bracing herself for more than the cold. She stared out at the oak, and her heart skipped a beat when he wasn't there.

Stepping forward on the porch, she strained her eyes to catch sight of him. And then, like a thief in the night, he was behind her, his strong arms encircling her waist and his lips lost in her hair. He was kissing her, whispering things that caused her cheeks to flame in the glow of the moonlight. The heat of his touch felt like fire. *Oh God, I need your help!*

And then, somewhere deep inside, beneath the passion he stirred, she could see things clearly once again. Yes, she wanted this—and she wanted it with him. But it had to be God's way, not hers and certainly not his.

With a calm not experienced in his presence before, Faith pried his arms from her waist and slowly turned, hands propped on his chest to push him away. The startled look on his face almost made her smile as she stepped back.

"It's you!" he muttered, clearly taken by surprise, and she noticed his reflexes were a bit slower than usual. The easy smile was conspicuously absent, and he seemed shaken.

"Did you think I was going to send my sister down? Are you crazy ... or just not very bright?" This was fun. It felt wonderful getting the best of Collin McGuire.

Julie Lessman

Collin blinked, and then instinct kicked in with the slow smile. His eyes traveled from her face, down her body, and back up again. Even in the moonlight, he could see her blush.

"No," he drawled, "I just thought you wanted me for yourself."

THE NON-KISS

Okay, I don't claim to be real good at scenes without kisses, but I gave it the old college try in *Love at Any Cost*, which I hope shows that romantic tension can be achieved *without* a lip lock. Gosh, who knew?! This scene takes place at the heroine's uncle's Napa estate during a game of Midnight (nighttime hide and seek).

Jamie ducked behind a massive rhododendron into Cassie's secret crevice, a narrow corridor created by a deep sun porch on the south side of Logan's estate. Lips easing into a grin, he inched several feet back to where she hid in the shadows with her back to the brick wall.

Even in the dark, he saw the whites of her eyes expand. "What are you doing here?" she whispered, shooing him away. "This is my hiding place, MacKenna—go!"

"Ten o'clock, eleven o'clock, midnight!" Liddy called.

Jamie chuckled. "Too late," he whispered, sandwiching himself behind her with his back to the wall. He looped an arm to her waist, tightening his hold to quiet her when a flicker of lamplight indicated someone just passed. Heady scents rose to taunt him—lilac water and Pear's soap mingling with the loamy scent of moss that never saw the light of day—delicious perfumes all, tingling his skin. His smile tipped at the soft absence of a corset that allowed him to feel the tension in her body along with the race of her pulse, evident in the rapid rise and fall of her chest.

Footsteps faded away, and she tried to whirl around, luring a grin to his lips when she got stuck halfway. "Jamie MacKenna," she hissed in the dark, "what in tarnation are you doing?"

Nudging her back around, he hooked her from behind once again, grazing her ear with a low chuckle. "This is my hiding place, Cowgirl. Can I help it if you stole it first?"

"Yours?!" she whispered loudly, her voice a near-squeak. "This has been my hiding place since I was knee-high to a grape, you pickle-brained polecat."

"I know," he said with a grin in his voice. "Blake told me."

She grunted and wrestled to get free. "Let-me-go! Have you forgotten our agreement?"

"No, ma'am." He firmed his grip, careful to brush his nose to the soft flesh of her lobe before he breathed warm in her ear. "No kisses are involved, Miss McClare," he said softly, taking her hand in his. His thumb teased the inside of her palm. "Hugs and hands only, I believe the fine print said." His fingers skimmed to her wrist, eyes closed to lose himself in the silky touch of her skin, the chaotic sprint of a pulse racing along with his own.

Her shuddery breaths filled the darkened space between them, matched by his own jagged breathing as he buried his face in her hair. "Cass," he whispered, unable to stop the heat that shimmered his skin. "I'm in love with you …"

THE STAKE-A-CLAIM KISS

In *A Passion Most Pure*, the second hero, Mitch Dennehy, has been a perfect gentleman with the heroine, Faith O'Connor, *until* he discovers she still has feelings for another man, which he attempts to dispel with a heated kiss.

When he took her home that night, he had given her his usual gentle kiss.

"I'll see you Monday," she whispered, pushing the door ajar.

Something inside had compelled him to pull her close. "No, you'll see me tonight, in your dreams, and that's an order. But just to make sure ..."

Never would he forget the look—eyes blinking wide as he dragged her to him, her soft lips parting in surprise as his mouth took hers with a hunger long suppressed. His hands wandered her back, urging her close while his lips roamed the curve of her neck, returning to reclaim her mouth with a fervor. For one brief, glorious moment, the terms were his, and by thunder, she would feel the heat of his kiss in her bones.

In a raspy gulp of air, she lunged back. "I can't believe you did that!" she gasped.

"Believe it," he quipped, his tone nonchalant.

"But, why? After what I told you tonight, why would you do that?"

"Why? Let's just call it a bit of insurance."

"What?"

"Insurance. If the woman I love is going to have memories of passion, it's going to be with me, not him."

"I don't entertain memories of passion." Her voice was edged with anger.

"You will tonight," he said. And turning on his heel, he left her—hopefully with a warmth that defied the coolness of the night.

THE SURROGATE KISS

In *A Passion Most Pure*, the hero, Collin McGuire, has feelings for the heroine, Faith O'Connor, that scare and upset him so much, he tries to drive her from her thoughts by kissing her sister.

"Charity, I made a promise to your parents. I need to win their trust ..."

She tossed her hair over her shoulder with the degree of defiance he'd always found so attractive. The look in her eyes was hard to miss. "What about my trust, Collin? Win mine!"

He hesitated and then slowly wrapped his arms around her waist. Her lips were warm and moist as he caressed them with his own, and their soft touch should have ignited a fire in him. Instead, a cold wave of fear crawled in his belly as he found himself aching for her sister. He could hear Charity's breathing, rapid and intense, the way his should have been, and the fear exploded into anger.

No! This was not happening! She was not going to do this to him. He was in control of his destiny. *He* would choose whom he'd love, not some make-believe god, and certainly not the woman who blindly gave her soul to him. Roughly he drew Charity in, kissing her with enough force to take her breath away. He felt a fire stir deep inside, and he kissed her again, pressing her close until his thoughts were consumed only with her.

Breathless, she leaned against his chest and gazed up at him. "I love you, Collin," she said, her eyes aglow with passion.

"I love you, too, Charity," he lied and kissed her again, putting to rest for the moment any doubts she might have had.

And there you have it—absolute proof that a kiss is *not* just a kiss ... it's chocolate to a romance-lover's soul!

Class dismissed!

A Note to My Readers

Thank you for joining me for **ROMANCE-ology 101**—I hope you enjoyed the class! If you did, please help other readers find this book via any of the following:

1. Word of mouth is crucial to an author, so if you found this book helpful, please spread the word!

2. If you enjoyed this book and found it helpful, please consider posting a review.

3. I encourage you to sign up for my bi-annual newsletter on my website at http://www.julielessman.com/sign-up-for-newsletter/, which will keep you apprised of important information about my books, such as release dates and freebie/reduced sales, sneak peeks at the publication process, covers, excerpts for each book, upcoming book signings, speaking engagements or blog interviews/giveaways, and information about current contests.

4. "Like" my Facebook page and follow me on Twitter.

5. Subscribe to my weekly blog, **Journal Jots**, which is a broad mix of what I'm up to including current info on my books, giveaways, fun things I'm doing, sneak peeks at new excerpts, personal glimpses into a writer's life, or just my own personal devotional for the day.

6. Subscribe to the **Seekerville** blog, a writer's blog of 13 Inspirational authors chosen by *Writer's Digest* as "101 Best Websites for Writers." Seekerville is a close-knit community of both writers and readers where our blogs inform, teach, inspire, motivate, and encourage writers on the road to publication and beyond. We are also the home to "Fifty Shades of Pray," Speedbo, The October Birthday Bash, Seekerville's 24-hour Rockin' New Years' Eve Party, Yankee Belle Café, and Seekerville the Town.

Thank you again for your support and God bless!

Hugs,
Julie

My Books

I invite you to get to know both the O'Connor family in The Daughters of Boston and Winds of Change series and The McClare family in the Heart of San Francisco series. Descriptions of each book can be found on the "Books" tab of my website at http://www.julielessman.com/books/, and excerpts of my favorite romantic and spiritual scenes are located on the "Excerpts" tab at http://www.julielessman.com/excerpts/.

The Daughters of Boston Series

Book 1: *A Passion Most Pure*
Amazon, Barnes & Noble, Books a Million,
Christian Book Distributors, Family Christian Stores, Lifeway

Book 2: *A Passion Redeemed*
Amazon, Barnes & Noble, Christian Stores, Books a Million, Christian Book Distributors, Family Christian Stores, Lifeway

Book 3: *A Passion Denied*
Amazon, Barnes & Noble, Books a Million, Christian Book Distributors, Family Christian Stores, Lifeway

Winds of Change Series

Book 1: *A Hope Undaunted*
Amazon, Barnes & Noble, Books A Million, Christian Book Distributors, Family Christian Stores, Lifeway

Book 2: *A Heart Revealed*
Amazon, Barnes & Noble, Books A Million, Christian Book Distributors, Family Christian Stores, Lifeway

Book 3: *A Love Surrendered*
Amazon, Barnes & Noble, Books A Million, Christian Book Distributors, Family Christian Stores, Lifeway

The Ebook Prequel

A Light in the Window: An Irish Love Story
Amazon, Barnes and Noble, Smashwords

The Heart of San Francisco Series

Book 1: *Love at Any Cost*
Amazon, Barnes & Noble, Berean Book Stores, Books A Million, Christian Book Distributors, Indiebound, Lifeway

Book 2: *Dare to Love Again*

Book 3: *Dare to Hope* (working title, release date 2014)

About the Author

Julie Lessman is an award-winning author whose tagline of "Passion with a Purpose" underscores her intense passion for both God and romance. Winner of the 2009 ACFW Debut Author of the Year and Holt Medallion Awards of Merit for Best First Book and Long Inspirational, Julie is also the recipient of 15 Romance Writers of America awards and was voted by readers as "Borders Best of 2009 So Far: Your Favorite Fiction."

Chosen as the #1 Romance Fiction Author of the Year in the *Family Fiction* magazine 2012 and 2011 Readers Choice Awards, Julie was also awarded #1 Historical Fiction Author of the Year in that same poll and #3 Author of the Year, #4 Novel of the Year and #3 Series of the year. Book 1 in her "Winds of Change" series, *A Hope Undaunted,* ranked on Booklist's Top 10 Inspirational Fiction for 2010. Her ebook *A Light in the Window* is an International Digital Awards winner, a 2013 Readers' Crown Award winner, and a 2013 Book Buyers Best Finalist.

Julie resides in Missouri with her husband and family and loves to hear from her readers, so please feel free to contact her through the following:

Her website at www.julielessman.com
On Facebook at http://www.facebook.com/pages/Julie-Lessman/98874268454
On Twitter at @julielessman
On the Seekerville blog at http://www.seekerville.blogspot.com/
Or on her personal blog, *Journal Jots,* at http://www.julielessman.com/journal-jots1/

Made in United States
Troutdale, OR
11/29/2023

14978338R00044